THRAXAS

THRAXAS

Martin Scott

ORBIT

An *Orbit* Book

First published in Great Britain by Orbit 1999

Copyright © Martin Scott 1999

The moral right of the author has been asserted.

A CIP catalogue record for this book
is available from the British Library.

ISBN 1 85723 729 3

Typeset by Solidus (Bristol) Ltd, Bristol
Printed and bound in Great Britain by
Mackays of Chatham plc, Chatham, Kent

Orbit
A Division of
Little, Brown and Company (UK)
Brettenham House
Lancaster Place
London WC2E 7EN

CHAPTER
ONE

Turai is a magical city. From the docks at Twelve Seas to Moon Eclipse Park, from the stinking slums to the Imperial Palace, a visitor can find all manner of amazing persons, astonishing items and unique services. You can get drunk and swap tales with Barbarian mercenaries in the dockside taverns, watch musicians, tumblers and jugglers in the streets, dally with whores in Kushni, transact business with visiting Elves in Golden Crescent, consult a Sorcerer in Truth is Beauty Lane, gamble on chariots and gladiators at the Stadium Superbius, hire an Assassin, eat, drink, be merry and consult an apothecary for your hangover. If you find a translator you can talk to the dolphins in the bay. If you're still in need of fresh experiences after all that, you could go and see the new dragon in the King's zoo.

If you have a problem, and you don't have much money, you can even hire me. My name is Thraxas. I've done all of the things mentioned above. Apart from the King's new dragon. I haven't seen that. I don't feel the urge. I saw enough dragons in the last Orc Wars.

I am forty-three, overweight, without ambition, and prone to prolonged bouts of drinking. The sign on my door mentions the word Sorcerer but my powers are of the lowest grade, mere tricks compared to the skills of

Turai's greatest. I am in fact a Private Investigator. Cheapest Sorcerous Investigator in the whole magical city of Turai.

When the situation is bad and the Civil Guard won't help, you can come to me. When what you really need is a powerful Sorcerer but if you can't afford to hire one, come to me. When an Assassin is on your tail and you want someone to serve as cannon fodder, come to me. If the city Consul isn't interested in your case and you've been ejected from the offices of the high-class Investigators uptown, I'm your man. Whatever people's problems are, when they've exhausted all other avenues and can't afford anything better, they come to me. Sometimes I'm able to help them. Sometimes not. Either way my finances never improve.

I used to work at the Imperial Palace. I was a Senior Investigator with Palace Security but I drank myself out of the job. That was a long time ago. No one there is much pleased to see me these days.

I live in two rooms above the Avenging Axe, a dockside tavern run by Gurd, an ageing northern Barbarian who used to fight for Turai as a mercenary. He was a good fighter. So was I. We fought alongside each other on many occasions, but we were a lot younger then. It's a lousy place to live but I can't afford anything better. There are no women in my life, unless you count Makri, who works as a barmaid downstairs and sometimes acts as my assistant. Makri, a strange bastard mix of Human, Elf and Orc, is a handy woman with a sword, and even the drunken lechers who frequent Gurd's tavern know better than to abuse her.

As far as I know, Makri has no romantic attachments,

though I've caught her a few times looking wistfully at some of the tall handsome Elves who occasionally pass through here on their way from the docks to Golden Crescent. No chance with them however. Makri's mongrel breeding makes her a social outcast practically everywhere. A pure-bred Elf wouldn't look at her twice, for all her youth and beauty.

I have no desire for any personal involvements, not since my wife ran off to the Fairy Glade with a Sorcerer's Apprentice half my age. Enough to put any man off. I wouldn't mind a client though. Funds are low and Gurd the Barbarian never likes it when his rent is late.

The Palace should hire me to find the missing Red Elvish Cloth. That's a big story in Turai just now, though they tried to keep it quiet. Red Elvish Cloth is more valuable than gold. I'd be in for a big reward if I found it. Unfortunately no one wants me. Palace Security and the Civil Guard are both on the case, and express every confidence that they'll locate it soon. I have every confidence they won't. Whoever was smart enough to hijack a load of heavily guarded Red Elvish Cloth on its way to the city is smart enough to hide it from the Guard.

CHAPTER
TWO

Early spring in Turai is temperate and pleasant, but brief. The long summer and autumn are unbearably hot. Every winter it rains continually for thirty days and thirty nights. After that it freezes so cold that beggars die in the streets. Which is enough about the climate for now.

The brief spring has ended and the temperature is starting to rise. Already I'm feeling uncomfortable, and I'm wondering if it's too early for my first beer of the day. Probably. I'm broke anyway. I haven't had a client in weeks. You might think that the crime rate in the city has dropped, except that crime in Turai never drops. Too many criminals, too much poverty, too many rich businessmen waiting to be robbed, or waiting to make an illegal profit. None of this money is coming my way however. The last time I worked I was successful, finding a magic amulet that old Gorsius Starfinder the Sorcerer mislaid during a drunken spree in a brothel. I recovered it and managed to keep the whole affair fairly quiet. His reputation at the Palace might suffer if his fondness for young prostitutes was too widely known.

Gorsius Starfinder promised to put a little business my way in return, but nothing has come of it. You can't really depend on a Palace Sorcerer to repay a favour. Too busy social climbing, drawing up horoscopes for young Princesses and that sort of thing.

I've just decided that there is really no alternative to going downstairs and having a beer, early or not, when there's a knock at my outside door. I have two rooms and use the outer one as an office. A staircase comes right up from the street for anyone who wishes to consult me without walking through the tavern.

'Come in.'

My rooms are very messy. I regret this. I never do anything about it.

The young woman who walks in looks like she might wrinkle her nose at anything less than a suite of rooms at the Palace. She pulls back her hood to reveal long golden hair, deep blue eyes and perfect features. Pretty as a picture, as we Investigators say.

'Thraxas, Private Investigator?'

I nod, and invite her to sit down, which she does after clearing some junk off a chair. We look at each other from opposite sides of the table over the remains of dinner from yesterday, or maybe the day before.

'I have a problem. Gorsius Starfinder told me that you may be able to help. He also told me you were discreet.'

'I am. But I think you might already have earned some attention coming down to Twelve Seas.'

I'm not referring to her beauty. I gave up complimenting young women on their beauty a long time ago. Around the time that my waistband expanded too much to make it worthwhile. But she is strikingly dressed, way too expensively for this miserable part of town. She's wearing a light black cloak trimmed with fur and under this she has a long blue velvet toga more suitable for dancing with courtiers in a ballroom than picking your way over the rotting fish heads in the street outside.

'My servant drove me here in a small cart. Covered. I don't think anyone saw me coming up the stairs. I wasn't quite prepared for—'

She waves her hand in a motion which covers both the state of my room and the street outside.

'Fine. How can I help?'

When an obviously wealthy young lady visits me, which is very seldom, I expect some reticence on her part. This is not unnatural, because such a person would only consult me if she's in some tight situation that she absolutely does not want any of her peers to know about, something so potentially embarrassing that she doesn't even want to risk going to a high-society Investigator up in Thamlin in case word leaks out. This young lady however is far from reticent and wastes no time getting to the point.

'I need you to recover a box for me. A small jewelled casket.'

'Someone steal it?'

'Not exactly.'

'What's in it?'

She hesitates. 'Do you need to know?'

I nod.

'Letters.'

'What sort of letters?' I ask.

'Love letters. From me. To a young attaché at the Niojan Embassy.'

'And you are?'

She pauses briefly, slightly surprised. 'I'm Princess Du-Akai. Don't you recognise me?'

'I don't get out much in high society these days.'

I suppose I should have recognised her from my work at the Palace, but the last time I saw her she was ten years old. I wasn't expecting the third in line to the Imperial Throne to waltz into my office. Imagine that. If King Reeth-Akan, Prince Frisen-Akan, and Prince Dees-Akan were all to die in an accident right this minute, I'd be sitting here talking to the new ruler of the city-state of Turai. Over a plate of three-day-old stew. Perhaps I should tidy my place more often.

'I take it your family would not be pleased to learn that you've been writing love letters to a young Niojan attaché?'

She nods.

'How many letters?'

'Six. He keeps them in a small jewelled box I gave him.'

'Why can't you just ask for it back?'

'Attilan – that's his name – refuses. Since I broke off our relationship he's been angry. But I had to. God knows what my father would have said if he'd learned of it. You understand this is very awkward. I can't ask Palace Security for help. The Royal Family has occasionally used Private Investigators for – other matters – but I can't take the risk of going anywhere I'll be known.'

I study her. She seems very calm, which surprises me. Young Princesses are not meant to write love letters. And not to Niojan diplomats of all people. Although there has been peace for a while now, Turai and our northern neighbour Nioj are historical enemies. Nioj is very strong and very aggressive and our King spends half his time desperately keeping the peace with them.

To make things worse, the Niojans are a deeply puritanical race, and their Church is particularly caustic about the state of the True Religion in Turai, always criticising something or other. Niojans are not the most popular of people in Turai.

If word of the affair leaked out there would be a terrible scandal. The public in this city loves a scandal. I still know enough about Palace politics to guess at what some of the factions would make of it. Senator Lodius, leader of the opposition party, the Populares, would exploit it as a means of discrediting the King. So I wonder a little about the Princess's apparent serenity. Perhaps our Royal Family are bred to control their emotions.

I take some details. I bump up my daily fee but even then I can tell she's shocked at how little I charge. Should have asked for more.

'I don't imagine it'll be too difficult, Princess. You mind spending a little money to get them back? I expect that's what he's after.'

She doesn't mind.

She asks me not to read the letters. I promise not to. She covers her head with her hood and departs.

My mood finally lightens. An easy enough case, in all likelihood, and I now have some money. It's lunchtime. I go downstairs for a beer. No reason not to. Perfectly respectable thing for a man to do after a hard morning's work.

THREE

The bar is full of dock workers and Barbarian mercenaries. The dockers drink here every lunchtime and the Barbarians are stopping off on their way to enlist in the army. All the tension between Turai and Nioj has led to heavy recruitment recently. There's trouble in the south as well, on the border with Mattesh. Some dispute about the silver mines. Turai belongs to a league of city-states with Mattesh and others, to defend us from the larger powers, but it's falling apart. Damned politicians. If they lead us into another war I'll be on the first horse out of town.

Gurd frowns at me. I give him some rent money. He smiles. He's a man of simple emotions, Gurd. I look round for Makri to see if she'll join me for a beer but she's too busy with the lunchtime trade, hurrying round the tables with her tray, collecting tankards and taking orders. Makri wears a tiny chainmail bikini at work, in keeping with the general 'Early Barbarian' decor that adorns Gurd's place, and as she has a particularly fine figure and the bikini exposes almost all of it she generally does well for tips.

Makri is a highly skilled swordswoman and if she was actually fighting you would never catch her in a chainmail bikini. She'd be dressed in full leather and steel body armour with a sword in one hand and an axe in the other and she'd have your head off your shoulders before you noticed whether she had a nice figure or not, but the bikini keeps the customers happy. Her long black hair hangs down over her dark, slightly reddish shoulders, her unusual skin colour the product of her Orc, Elf and Human parentage.

It's actually regarded as virtually impossible to carry the blood of all three races. The extremely few people who do so are considered freaks and outcasts from society. In the smarter areas of Turai Makri would not even be allowed into a tavern. Makri gets a lot of abuse about her parentage. On the streets children taunt her with 'half-breed', 'triple-breed', 'Orc bastard' and much worse.

I notice her slipping some bread from behind the bar to Palax and Kaby, a young pair of travelling musicians who've recently moved to the neighbourhood. They're good musicians, but busking brings in little money in a poor place like this, and they're looking hungry.

'Never like to see a man drinking alone,' says Partulax, joining me.

I nod. I have no objection to drinking on my own but I'm happy enough to have Partulax's company. He's a big red-haired man who used to drive wagons between the docks and the warehouses up in Koota Street. Now he's a paid official in the Transport Guild. I've worked for him once or twice on small matters.

'How's work?' I ask him.

'Okay. Better than rowing a slave galley.'

'How's things with the Guild?'

'Trade's good, wagons are full but we're having a hard time keeping the Brotherhood at bay.'

I nod. The Brotherhood, the main criminal fraternity in the south of the city, is always trying to make inroads on the labour guilds. Probably the craftsmen's guilds as well. Maybe even the Honourable Association of Merchants for all I know. The Brotherhood seems to be all-pervasive these days. More troublesome too. There have been numerous gang fights and killings involving them and the Society of Friends, the criminal organisation operating in the north of Turai. Most of the disputes revolve around control of the dwa trade. Dwa is a powerful and popular drug and there's a lot of money to be made out of it. The Brotherhood and the Society of Friends are not the only organisations angling for their share. Plenty of otherwise respectable people make a good living from dwa, even though it's illegal. The Civil Guard doesn't seem to do anything about it. Bribery works well in Turai.

'You hear about the new dragon?' says Partulax.

I nod. It was in the news-sheets.

'I hauled it up to the Palace.'

'How do you transport a dragon?'

'Carefully,' replies Partulax, and guffaws. 'It was asleep most of the time. The Orcs sent a keeper who drugged it.'

I frown. The dragon story is a bit weird when you think about it. The King has one dragon in his zoo and the Orcs have now lent him another one to mate with it. Very kind of them. Except Orcs don't perform acts of kindness for Humans. They hate us just as much as we hate them, even if we are technically at peace right now. Partulax, another veteran of the last war, doesn't know what to make of it either.

'You can't trust an Orc.'

I nod. You can't actually trust most Humans either, and the Elves aren't a hell of a lot better when it comes right down to it, but we old soldiers like to air our prejudices.

The bar empties as the dockers in their red bandannas make their way back to their afternoon shifts in the cargo holds, casting not a few backward glances at Makri's bikini-clad figure. Makri, ignoring their stares and comments, comes over to my table.

'Any progress?' she asks.

'Yes,' I reply. 'Got a case. Paid Gurd the rent.'

She frowns. 'That's not what I mean.'

I know it's not what she means, but what she means is a difficult proposition. Makri wishes to study at the Imperial University and she wants me to help her. This, as I have pointed out on numerous occasions, is impossible. The Imperial University is a deeply conservative body and does not accept female students. Even if it did, it would not accept a student with Orcish blood in her veins. Completely out of the question. The aristocrats and rich merchants who send their sons there would be up in arms. Questions would be asked in the Senate. The Turai news-sheets would create a scandal. Apart from all this Makri doesn't even have the basic academic qualifications necessary for entry.

Makri scoffs at these objections. She claims that it's well known that any student can get into the University, no matter how sparse their qualifications, providing they have a rich father to pay their fees or wield influence at the Palace.

'And anyway, I'm going to philosophy night classes at the Revered Federation of Guilds College. I'll get the qualifications.'

'The University doesn't teach women.'

'Neither did the College till I insisted. And don't go on about my parentage, I've had enough of that today from the customers. You promised you'd ask Astrath Triple Moon to help me.'

'I was drunk when I promised,' I protest. 'Anyway, Astrath couldn't help.'

'He's a Sorcerer. He must know people.'

'He's a Sorcerer in disgrace. None of his old friends would do him any favours.'

'Well, it would be a start,' says Makri with the look of a woman who is not going to stop harassing me until I give in. I give in.

'Okay, Makri. I'll talk to him.'

'You promise?'

'I promise.'

'Well you'd better then, or I'll be down on you like a bad spell.'

I ask Makri if she wants a drink but she still has a load of tables to clean so I take a beer upstairs and finish it off while I'm getting dressed to go out. I put on my best black tunic, which is patched, but quite professionally, and my best boots, which are a mess. One of the heels is about to come off. Not very impressive for visiting a Niojan diplomat. Staring in the bronze mirror I have to admit that I'm looking a little shabby these days. Altogether not too impressive. My hair is fine, still dark and long, and my moustache is as impressive as ever, but I've put on weight recently. In addition to my expanding waistline I seem to be getting a double chin. I sigh. Middle age.

I tie my hair back in a braid and hunt around for my

sword. I remember I pawned it last week to buy food. What sort of Private Investigator pawns his sword, for God's sake? Turai's cheapest, that's what sort.

I consider looking into the kuriya pool, but decide against it. The ability to use kuriya is one of my few claims to sorcerous power. It involves entering a trance and staring into a small pool of kuriya, a rare dark liquid, wherein may appear mystical insights. In a saucer full of kuriya I have occasionally been able to find the solution to an investigation – a missing husband, a thieving nephew, a lying business partner. Very convenient. Solve a mystery in the comfort of your own room. Unfortunately it rarely works. Using magic to draw a picture of the past is extremely difficult. Even Sorcerers with a great deal more power than myself are only sometimes successful. It requires precise calculations of the phases of the three moons and suchlike, and entering the required trance is no easy feat. The Investigating Sorcerers of the Civil Guard will generally only attempt it in the most important criminal matters, and fortunately for Turai's criminals they often get it wrong.

Another problem is the price of kuriya. The black liquid comes from the far west and the one merchant who imports it keeps his prices high. He claims it's dragon's blood, but he's a liar.

I place the sleep spell in my memory. I can only put one spell in at a time these days, and even that takes a lot of effort. Major spells don't stay in the memory after you've used them, so you have to learn them all over again. If I'm out on a case and think I may need a little outside help I usually memorise the sleep spell, but I find the whole process pretty tiring these days. I'm not much of a Sorcerer. No wonder I have to work for a living. A good Sorcerer can carry two major spells at once. A truly great one can walk around all day with three or even four spells safely tucked up in his memory, just waiting to come out. I should have studied more when I was an apprentice.

I step through the outside door and get to work. I mutter my standard locking incantation over the door, this being a minor spell which I'm able to use at will. Quite a number of people can use these minor spells. They don't require much studying.

'That's not going to help you much if you don't pay Yubaxas what you owe him,' comes a rasping voice from the bottom of the stairs.

I glower down at the large man who's waiting there for me. He's very tall, very broad, and a virulent sword scar runs from his temple to his collar bone. With his shaved head he's an ugly brute by anyone's standards, and one I'd rather not have hanging around to see me. I go down the stairs and stop on the third from the ground so that our eyes are level.

'What do you want, Karlox?' I demand.

'Passing on a message from Yubaxas. Money's due in five days.'

As if I needed reminding. Yubaxas is the local Brotherhood boss. I owe him five hundred gurans, a gambling debt after some very unwise speculations at the chariot races.

'He'll get his money,' I grunt. 'I don't need gorillas like you to remind me.'

'You better come up with it, Thraxas, or we'll be down on you like a bad spell.'

I push my way past. Karlox laughs. He acts as an enforcer for the Brotherhood and he's a violent and unpleasant man. He's also dumb as an Orc. No doubt he enjoys his work. I leave him without a backward glance. The gambling debt is worrying me, but I'm not going to let an ox like Karlox see that.

The air stinks of rotting fish. It's hotter than Orcish hell out here. I redeem my sword at Priso's pawn shop. I'd like a new pair of boots but I can't afford it. Nor can I afford to redeem my illuminated staff or my spell protection charm. I get depressed about my poverty. I shouldn't gamble. I should have stayed at the Palace, riding around in official horse carts and raking in bribes. I was a fool to leave. Or rather I was a fool to get so drunk at the wedding of the Head of Palace Security that I tried to make a move on his bride. No one at the Palace could ever remember an Investigator being dismissed from his post quite so abruptly, not even proven spies and traitors. Damn that Deputy Consul Rittius. He always hated me.

I buy some bread at Minarixa's bakery. Minarixa greets me in a friendly manner as I am a very frequent customer. Outside I notice she's put up a wall poster asking for donations to the Association of Gentlewomen. Quite a bold move on her part; many people disapprove of the Association of Gentlewomen, an unofficial organisation, deeply frowned on by the King, the Palace, the Senate, the Church, the guilds and practically every man in the city.

'A sinful thing,' says a voice beside me.

It's Derlex, the local Pontifex, or priest of the True Church.

I greet him politely, if slightly dubiously. I always feel

nervous around Derlex. I get the impression he disapproves of me.

'You don't sympathise with their aims, Pontifex Derlex?'

He doesn't. A women's organisation is anathema to the True Church. The young Pontifex seems quite upset by it. Not only does he dislike the poster, he doesn't seem to approve of Minarixa's bakery.

'Women should not run businesses,' he states.

As Minarixa runs the only decent bakery in the whole of Twelve Seas I can't agree with this at all, but I keep my silence. I don't want to argue with the Church, it's too powerful to offend.

'I haven't seen you at church recently,' says Derlex, taking me by surprise.

'Pressure of work,' I reply, foolishly, which gets me a lecture about putting my work before the Church.

'I'll certainly make every effort to attend this week,' I say as convincingly as I can, and make my escape. I can't say I enjoyed the conversation. The Pontifex isn't all that bad, provided he leaves you alone, but it's not going to be much fun if he suddenly starts worrying about my soul.

CHAPTER
FOUR

I step over three young dwa addicts lying unconscious in an alleyway. I sigh. The opening up of the southern trade route through Mattesh was proclaimed by our King as a triumph of diplomacy. Commerce has started to flow but unfortunately the main import has been dwa. Use of the powerful narcotic is now rife throughout the city and the effect on its population has been dramatic. Beggars, sailors, youthful apprentices, whores, itinerants, rich and idle young fashionables – all manner of people, once content to alleviate their sufferings with ale and occasional doses of the much milder drug Thazis, now spend their days lost in the powerful dream brought on by the ingestion of dwa. Unfortunately dwa is both expensive and addictive. Once you've taken your dose you're as happy as an Elf in a tree, but when you come down you feel dreadful. Those regular users who spend part of their lives lost in its pleasant grip are obliged to spend the other part raising money to buy their next day's supply. Since dwa swept Turai crime of all sorts has mushroomed. In many parts of the city it's not safe to walk the streets at night for fear of violent robbery. The houses of the rich are ringed by walls and guarded by hired members of the Securitus Guild. Gangs of youths in the slums who used to steal the occasional piece of fruit from market stalls now use knives for street robberies and kill people for a few gurans.

Turai is rotting. The poor are despairing and the rich are decadent. One day King Lamachus of Nioj will come down from the north and sweep us away.

I feel better when I've got my sword tucked snugly in my belt and I'm riding in a horse cab, or landus, up Moon and Stars Boulevard, the main street running north to south, up from Twelve Seas docks through Pashish, a poor though generally peaceful area, eventually turning on to Royal Way, which runs west through the upper-class suburb of Thamlin to the Imperial Palace. Attilan, our Royal Princess's erstwhile lover, lives here on a quiet street popular with young men about town.

I'm prepared to dislike him. Niojans are never friendly to Private Investigators. Private Investigators are in fact illegal in Nioj. Most things are illegal in Nioj. It's a grim place. Thamlin isn't. Our well-off citizens make their surroundings very comfortable – yellow and green tiled pavements and large white houses with fountains in well-tended gardens. Civil Guardsmen patrol the streets, keeping them safe from undesirables. It's a peaceful place. I used to live here. Some time ago. My old house is now occupied by the Queen's Royal Astrologer. He's a dwa addict, but he keeps it quiet.

A young Pontifex greets me politely as I turn into Attilan's private pathway. He's carrying a bag marked with the sign of the True Church. Busy gathering contributions from our wealthier citizens I expect. A servant answers the door. Attilan is not home and is not expected back in the near future. The servant shuts the door. I never enjoy having doors slammed in my face. I walk round the back. No one interrupts me as I stroll through the small garden, ending up in a patio at the back with a small statue of Saint Quatinius and various well-tended bushes. The back door is solid enough, and locked. I mutter the opening incantation, another minor spell which I can use at will, and it flies open. I walk in. I can guess the layout of the house. They're all much the same, with a central courtyard containing an altar and private rooms at the back. If, as I suspect, Attilan only has one or two servants, and they're lounging in their quarters while he's away, I may be able to carry out some uninterrupted investigating.

Attilan's office is neat, everything in its proper place. I check the letter rack. No sign of the Princess's letters. A safe behind a painting almost resists my opening spell, but eventually creaks open reluctantly. I might have made a fine burglar, although anyone with anything really valuable to hide gets their safe locked tight with a good spell from a competent Sorcerer. Inside the safe I find a jewelled box with the Princess's royal insignia on it. Very good. Things are going well.

I am about to place it in my bag when my curiosity overwhelms me. The Princess specifically requested that I did not open the box and read her letters. Which gives me an irresistible urge to open the box and read her letters. Sometimes I just can't help myself.

It doesn't appear to contain any letters. Just a parchment with a spell written on it. I frown. This is definitely the box the Princess asked me to retrieve; it carries her royal insignia. The spell is an unfamiliar one, not native to Turai. When I read it through I'm more puzzled than ever. It seems to be a spell for putting a dragon to sleep. Why would the Princess want to do that? I slip it into my bag, and hurry out the back way. It should be an easy getaway but as I plunge through the bushes I trip over something and cry out in surprise.

'Who's there?' demands a servant, appearing at a run. He stares in horror at me. Or rather, at what's at my feet, which is a dead body.

'Attilan!' he screams.

The case just took a bad turn. The servant obviously regards me as the man responsible for sticking a knife in his employer. So do the Civil Guards, who appear in less than thirty seconds. Not unreasonable, I suppose, as I decline to offer any explanation for my presence. They drag me off. As I'm being hauled through the garden I sense the faintest aura of something unusual but it's too fleeting to identify and I don't have a chance to think about it. I'm dumped in a wagon and driven smartly up to the prison. As the Guards fling me in a cell, I reflect that, of all my reversals of fortune, this is surely one of the quickest.

CHAPTER
FIVE

The city is divided into ten administrative units, each one overseen by a Prefect, who, among other things, oversees the Civil Guard in his area. Prefect Galwinius, in charge of Thamlin, is a large, tough individual who wastes no time in informing me I'm in serious trouble.

'We got no time for Private Investigators round here,' he snarls at me, again. 'Why did you kill Attilan?'

'I didn't kill him.'

'Then why were you there?'

'Just taking a short cut.'

I'm flung back in my cell. It's stiflingly hot and stinks like a sewer. Out of curiosity I try my standard opening incantation on the door, but nothing happens. This is to be expected. All cell doors are regularly serviced by the Civil Guard Sorcerers using powerful locking spells.

Hours pass. I hear the Crier calling Sabap, the time for afternoon prayer. At this all faithful members of the True Church – in theory the whole population of the city – are supposed to get down on their knees and pray. Pray for the second time, as all true devotees will also have prayed at Sabam, the start of the day. I missed the morning prayers. Didn't wake up in time. I haven't done in years. I decide to pass on the afternoon session as well.

The door rattles and Captain Rallee strides in.

'Don't you know all citizens are legally obliged to pray during Sabap?' he says.

'I don't see you on your knees.'

'I'm excepted for official business.'

'What business?'

'Coming down to order you to stop being such a fool and tell the Prefect what he wants to know.'

It's some relief to see Captain Rallee, though not much. We've known each other a long time; we even fought in the same battalion during one of the Orc Wars. We were fairly friendly once, but since I left the Palace and set up on my own we've grown apart. He knows I'm not a fool but he doesn't owe me any favours.

'Look, Thraxas, we don't want to keep you here. We've got better things to do. No one thinks you personally stuck a knife in Attilan.'

'Prefect Galwinius does.'

Captain Rallee makes a face indicating he doesn't think too much of the Prefect.

'We ran a test on the knife. Our Sorcerer reports that your aura isn't on it. Of course some Sorcerers could remove their aura, but you aren't good enough to do that.'

'Absolutely, Captain. I'm strictly small time.'

'But he picked up your aura in the house. What were you doing there?'

I continue staring at the ceiling.

'You know how serious this is, Thraxas? Attilan was a Niojan diplomat. Their Ambassador is raising hell. The Palace is raising hell. The Consul himself's been down here asking questions.'

I'm impressed. The Consul is Turai's highest official,

answerable to no one except the King. Captain Rallee stares at me. I stare at him. He's weathered his middle age better than I have. With his long blond hair and broad shoulders he's still a handsome man. Probably still a hit with the ladies, in his smart black tunic and cloak. No fool, though. Sharp as an Elf's ear in comparison to some of the blunderers they've got in the Civil Guard.

'So what's going on?'

I remain silent.

'I don't reckon you killed Attilan,' says the Captain. 'But I reckon you might have been involved in a little robbery.'

'Don't be stupid.'

'Stupid? Maybe. Maybe not. I've never known you rob anyone before, but then again, I've never known you owe the Brotherhood five hundred gurans before.'

He sees my look of surprise.

'You're in big trouble, Thraxas. Yubaxas will have your head if you don't pay. You need money badly, which naturally makes us suspicious when you're found in rich people's houses where you haven't been invited. So why don't you tell me what's going on?'

'I don't discuss my business with the Civil Guard. Or anyone else. If I did, I'd soon be out of clients.'

'Who's your client?'

'I don't have one.'

'In that case, Thraxas, you'd better reconsider your attitude to prayer. Unless you tell us what we want to know it's going to take divine intervention to get you out of this cell.'

He departs. I remain. Languishing, I believe would be the correct term.

Later I bribe a jailer to let me have a news-sheet.

The Renowned and Truthful Chronicle of All the World's Events is one of the various rags published each day in Turai. It's neither renowned nor truthful, being given more to hinting at scandalous relationships between Senators' daughters and officers of the Palace Guard, but it's entertaining. It's a single sheet, poorly printed, and often contains nothing but gossip, but today it has the sensational news of Attilan's death, about which the Niojan Ambassador is indeed raising hell. He has protested to the King about this gross breach of diplomatic privilege. He has a point. You can't have your diplomatic privilege violated much more than being murdered. For our King, always keen to appease the Niojans, it's a tricky situation, and the Palace needs the murder cleared up quickly. Quickly enough to pin it on me, quite possibly.

Thinking it over in my cell, I can't make much sense of the affair. I've no idea who killed Attilan. Or why the Princess sent me to recover some love letters which turned out to be a spell for putting a dragon to sleep. Who needs to do that? There are no dragons around, apart from the King's pet in his zoo, and the new one from the Orcs. I muse about this. It's an interesting tale. This dragon, newly arrived at the King's zoo, was on loan. The Orcish nation of Gzak sent it to King Reeth-Akan last week to mate with the King's dragon as a token of friendship. There is, of course, no friendship whatsoever between Turai and Gzak, or any Human and Orcish nation, peace treaties notwithstanding. Why exactly the Orcs have sent it I'm not sure. I doubt very much that they are overly concerned that King Reeth-Akan's dragon might be feeling lonely. Maybe it's just to fool people into thinking they aren't planning another war as soon as they can get their armies up to strength after the last beating we gave them. Gzak is one of the richest Orcish nations and has its own gold and diamond mines. It won't take them too many years to build up their strength again.

Why, however, Princess Du-Akai might want to put this or any other dragon to sleep is a mystery.

I glance at the rest of the news-sheet. Usual round of Palace intrigue and scandal, and a story about a killer called Sarin the Merciless who's apparently carried out a string of murders and robberies in the southern nations, making her the most wanted criminal in the west. This makes me laugh. I tangled with Sarin the Merciless a long time ago. Ran her out of town, if the truth be known. Just another small-time crook. The news-sheets always like to build up these petty criminals into something they're not. I hope she comes back to Turai. I could do with some reward money.

Under this is a piece about Senator Lodius, the leader of the opposition, who is haranguing the Consul for the outbreak of lawlessness in Turai. Killings and robberies are on the rise, and there's still no sign of the Red Elvish Cloth, for which the Treasury will have to pay the Elves, even though we haven't got it.

What makes this cloth so rare and valuable is its ability to form a total shield against magic. It's the only substance in the world no sorcery can penetrate. Very handy in a world full of enemy Sorcerers. But it's presumably far away from the city by now. If it had been brought to Turai by the hijackers, our government

Sorcerers would have traced it by now. In its finished
state, the cloth is undetectable, but Elves aren't dumb.
Any time they despatch some, they brand it with a
temporary sorcerous mark only they can remove. Once
the Cloth reaches our King, an Elvish Sorcerer removes
it. So someone has spirited the stuff away from the city.
It's well known the Orcs have been after Red Elvish Cloth
for years. If they've finally acquired some, it's bad news
for us.

My musings are interrupted as the cell door bangs
open and the jailer ushers in a young woman. She
introduces herself as Jaisleti and flashes an official seal
at me.

'I'm Princess Du-Akai's handmaiden.'

'Whisper. You never know who's listening.'

Jaisleti whispers, 'The Princess is worried.'

'It's okay. I hid the box before I was arrested. I've kept
her name out of it.'

Jaisleti looks relieved. 'When can she get the letters
back?'

'As soon as I get out of here.'

'We'll see what we can do. But you mustn't mention
her name. Now Attilan's been murdered it would be an
even worse scandal if the relationship were to be
discovered.'

'Don't worry. Stubborn silence is one of my strongest
points.'

She departs, sticking to the pretence about love
letters. No mention of dragons at all.

CHAPTER
SIX

The call for Sabav, evening prayers, rings out through the jail. Sabam, Sabap, Sabav. Three prayer calls a day. Gets me down. Still, we get off lightly in Turai. In Nioj they have six. I kneel down to pray in case some jailer is spying on me; there's no sense in giving the authorities another excuse to hold me here. Perhaps it isn't such a bad idea, because I'm released shortly afterwards. God may now be on my side. More likely the Princess pulled some strings. Captain Rallee is most displeased. He can't understand how a guy like me can still have any influence in this town.

'Who you working for, the Royal Family?' he grumbles, as a Sorcerer mutters the spell to let me out the front gates. 'You watch yourself, Thraxas. The Prefect's got his eye on you. You try putting anything over on him and he'll be down on you like a bad spell.'

I smile graciously in reply, and climb into a landus heading for Twelve Seas. I stop off at the public baths, wash off the stink of prison, grab a beer and food at the Avenging Axe and head off out.

'Where have you been?' asks Makri as I'm leaving.

'In prison.'

'Oh,' says Makri. 'I thought maybe you were hiding from the Brotherhood.'

I glare at her. 'And why did you think that?'

'Because you can't pay your gambling debts.'

I am outraged to learn that Makri knows about this too.

'Does everyone in Twelve Seas have to stick their noses into my personal affairs? It's high time people around here started minding their own damned business.'

With which I storm out into the street. A beggar sticks a withered hand in my direction.

'Get a job,' I bark at him. It makes me feel slightly better.

It's dark by the time I reach Attilan's house. It's risky returning so soon but it has to be done. In the time between my discovery in the garden and my arrest, I threw the box under a bush and I need it back. No one seems to be around, apart from a young Pontifex hurrying home after a hard day's praying. I wish I could make myself invisible but the invisibility spell is way too complicated for me. Trusting to luck, I haul myself over the fence, scramble through the garden and dive beneath the bush. The box isn't there. Someone beat me to it. Two minutes later I'm back over the fence and hurrying south, not pleased at the way things are going.

Horse traffic is banned in the city after dark. The night is still hot and it's a tiring walk. When I reach Pashish I decide to drop in on Astrath Triple Moon. I've promised Makri I'll ask him if he can help her. More to the point, I need a beer.

Pashish, just north of Twelve Seas, is another poor suburb, though relatively crime-free. Its narrow tenemented streets comprise mainly the dwellings of harbour workers and other manual labourers. It's an unlikely place to find a Sorcerer, but Astrath Triple Moon is somewhat of an outcast among his kind, thanks to certain allegations a few years back when he was the official Sorcerer at the Stadium Superbius, with responsibility for ensuring that all chariot races and suchlike were run fairly, without outside sorcerous interference. Certain powerful Senators felt that their chariots weren't getting a fair deal, leading to a Praetor's investigation accusing Astrath Triple Moon of taking bribes.

Astrath employed me to dig up evidence on his behalf. He was, in fact, as guilty as hell but I managed to cloud the issue enough for him to escape prosecution or expulsion from the Sorcerers Guild. This allowed him to remain in the city – no Sorcerer expelled from the Guild is allowed to practise here – but the stigma attached to his name thereafter forced him to leave his high-class practice in Truth is Beauty Lane. He ended up in straitened circumstances with a small practice in Pashish ministering to the humble needs of the local population.

Astrath is still a powerful Sorcerer. As always he is pleased to see me. Not many men of my learning and culture visit him these days. He pours me a beer and I down it in one. He pours me another.

'Hot as Orcish hell out there,' I say, emptying the glass.

He pours me a third. He's not a bad guy for a Sorcerer. I dump my cloak and bag on the floor among the astrolabes, charts, test tubes, herbs, potions and books that form the standard paraphernalia of a working Sorcerer.

I ask him about the spell, describing it as best as I can remember.

'That's a rare item,' says Astrath Triple Moon, stroking his beard. 'As far as I know, no Human Sorcerer has ever concocted a successful spell for putting a dragon to sleep. The best we've come up with is some temporary distraction.'

He's right. I know from painful experience. My platoon faced a dragon in the last Orc Wars, and I tried my sleep spell, full strength. I had more power in my spells then but the dragon hardly blinked. Still, we killed it in the end.

'Do the Orcs have a spell like that?'

'They might,' replies Astrath Triple Moon. 'After all, they have more experience with dragons than us. And their Sorcerers work on a different system. Weaker in some ways, stronger in others. It wouldn't surprise me if they've mastered dragoncraft enough to put one to sleep. I wouldn't have thought they'd let a spell like that out of their hands though. There's always Horm, of course.'

'Horm the Dead?'

I suppress a shudder. You can forget to include me in anything involving Horm the Dead. He's not the only mad renegade Sorcerer in the world but he's one of the most powerful and, by all accounts, by far the most frightening.

'You ever have any dealings with him?'

Astrath strokes his beard.

'Not really. But a few members of the Sorcerers Guild have encountered him in the course of their travels and they told me stories about him. That was back when I could still go to Sorcerers Guild meetings of course. Takes dwa and flies, apparently.'

'So do a lot of people.'

'No, he really can fly. So they say anyway. And rides dragons.'

'I thought only Orcs could ride dragons.'

'Horm is half Orc,' says Astrath. 'And he spends his time in the Wastelands working out ways to combine Orc and Human magic. Last we heard he was working on a spell to send a whole city mad. The Eight-Mile Terror, he called it. So we were told anyway. Of course, you can't trust informants from the Wastelands, but it worried the Guild enough to start work on some counterspell. Horm the Dead doesn't much care for Humans.'

'I can't see why he'd have any involvement in this spell the Princess had though.'

'Neither can I,' admits Astrath Triple Moon. 'And from what you can remember of the spell, it doesn't really sound like his work. More likely it was stolen from an Orcish Sorcerer. Or maybe their Ambassadors brought it here just in case the dragon decided to go mad and start burning the city.'

I should hurry home and work this one out. After another beer, a little klee, and a portion of beef from Astrath's servant, I do just that. I sit in my shabby room and mull it over. What would a Niojan diplomat be doing with an Orcish spell? Trying to sell it perhaps? A valuable item, certainly, which any government would pay well for, but how did he get it? How did the Princess learn of it and why did she want it? And where is it now? Who removed it from Attilan's garden?

Faced with so many questions, I go downstairs for a beer. Makri comes over to my table and I tell her about the case. She's a sensible woman, often good for talking things over with, providing she's not haranguing me about helping her get into the Imperial University.

'I don't think Attilan was ever on diplomatic duty in the Orcish lands, but its possible he's come across the Orcish diplomats at our Palace. They don't show themselves in public but they must meet other Ambassadors sometimes.'

'Maybe he didn't steal it,' suggests Makri. 'Maybe they gave it to him.'

'Seems unlikely, Makri. Niojans are all swines, but they don't like Orcs any more than we do. And even if he was working with them, what was he doing with that spell? And why is the Princess involved? She sent me to find it. How did she know he had it? And what did she want it for?'

'Maybe the dragons in the King's zoo make her nervous.'

'Could be. Dragons would upset anyone.'

'I fought one once,' says Makri.

'What?'

'I fought one. In the Orcish slave arena.'

'On your own?'

'No, there were ten of us. Big fight to entertain the Orc Lords. We beat it, though I was the only one left alive at the end. Tough skin. My sword wouldn't go through it. I had to stab it in the eyes.'

I stare at her. I'm not sure if she's telling the truth or not. When the twenty-year-old Makri arrived in Turai a year ago after escaping from the Orcish gladiator slave pits, she was a hardened fighter but unused to the ways of civilisation. That is to say, she didn't tell lies. After a year in the Avenging Axe, surrounded by notable embroiderers of the truth like Gurd and myself, she's learned the art.

'I fought a dragon too, back in the Orc Wars,' I say, which is true, though rather beside the point. I just don't like Makri to think she's the only one round here who's done any serious fighting.

Some customers call for beer. Makri ignores them.

'I hope you're not going to get Princess Du-Akai into trouble,' she says.

'Why?'

'Because if you do a good job for the Princess she'll be grateful and you could ask her to use her influence to get me into the University.'

The standard degree course at the Imperial University features rhetoric, philosophy, logic, mathematics, architecture, religion and literature. Why the hell Makri wants to learn all that is beyond me.

'Also,' adds the young Barbarian, 'I heard that Du-Akai is sympathetic to the Association of Gentlewomen.'

'Where did you hear that?'

'At a meeting.'

I stare at her. I'd no idea Makri was going to Association of Gentlewomen meetings.

'Don't come crying to me if you all get arrested for illegal gatherings.'

'I won't.'

I consider consulting the kuriya pool for some answers but decide against it. I don't know enough exact dates and places for the things I'd like to know, so a good connection with the past would be almost impossible. Anyway I've hardly any of the black liquid left and I can't afford any more. Sorcerous Investigator. Big joke. I can't even afford the basics.

'Get a job,' says Makri.

'Very funny. You want to play some niarit after your shift?'

Makri nods. She tells me she saw some Elves today, travelling up from the docks on horseback with an escort of Civil Guardsmen.

'Probably some deputation from the Elf Lord who sent the Red Elvish Cloth. I don't imagine they're very happy it's gone missing.'

Makri grunts. The whole subject of Elves is troubling to her. Basically, her Orcish blood appals them. Makri pretends not to care, but really she does. She won't admit it, but I've seen her looking almost longingly at some of the young Elves who pass through Twelve Seas.

She adjusts her bikini and gets back to work, taking orders from thirsty late-night drinkers. This includes me and it's around two in the morning by the time I stumble upstairs.

Sitting on my grubby couch is Princess Du-Akai.

'I let myself in,' she says. 'I didn't want to come into the tavern.'

'Feel free to visit any time,' I grunt, with less politeness than would be normal towards the third in line to the throne. I'm not particularly pleased to find anyone, even a Royal Princess, in my rooms uninvited. It gives me the strong suspicion she might have been searching them.

'Did you get the box?'

I shake my head. 'I went back for it. Someone must have seen me hide it. It's gone.'

'I must have those letters!'

I stare at the Princess. For the first time she looks uncomfortable. Good. I decide to give it to her straight.

'There weren't any letters, Princess. Your box was

there in Attilan's safe all right. Nice box. Very fine inlay.
No letters though. Just an Orc spell for putting a dragon
to sleep.'

'How dare you examine the contents!'

'Welcome to the real world. And how dare you send
me on a case with false information. Thanks to you,
Princess, I'm up to my neck in the murder of a Niojan
diplomat. Sure, you used your influence to get me out of
prison but that's not going to prevent the Consul pinning
the murder on me if no one better comes along. So I'd
suggest you start telling me the truth.'

We stare at each other for a while. Princess Du-Akai
shows no inclination to start telling the truth.

'Do you know who killed Attilan?' I demand.

'No.'

'Did you?'

She's shocked. She denies it.

'Why did you want me to get that spell? Where did it
come from? And why was it in your box?'

The Princess clams up. She makes to leave. I'm mad as
hell. Anytime I'm thrown in a cell I at least like to know
the reason. I say a few less than complimentary things to
her. She tosses a small purse on the table and tells me our
business relationship is ended.

'Don't slam the door when you leave.'

She slams the door. I count the money. Thirty gurans.
Three days' pay. Not bad. Another four hundred and
seventy and the Brotherhood will be off my back. I wish I
knew what it had all been about. I drink some more beer.
It feels too hot to go to bed. I fall asleep on my couch.

CHAPTER
SEVEN

I'm woken about three thirty in the morning by Makri. 'Makri, how many times do I have to tell you not to barge into my rooms? I might be doing something personal.'

She laughs at the thought.

'I'm going to start putting a closing spell on that door.'

'Your closing spell wouldn't hold out for fifteen seconds against me, Thraxas.'

I expect it wouldn't. Makri started fighting in the slave pits when she was thirteen. Seven years as an Orcish gladiator does give a person a tendency to be forceful. I struggle to rise as Makri clears some space on an old box to set up my niarit board.

'What's the matter with you?' she asks. 'You're looking sadder than a Niojan whore.'

I tell her what happened with the Princess. 'I got three days' pay but I was hoping for a lot more. I guess she won't hire me again after this. And I wouldn't count on her help getting into the University.'

'You mean you insulted her?'

I admit it, but point out it was justified.

Makri takes out a couple of thazis sticks.

'This'll cheer you up.'

'If Gurd catches you taking them from the bar you'll be out on your ear.'

She shrugs. I light my thazis stick.

'How's your studies at the Guild College?' I ask.

'Okay. Better than rowing a slave galley.'

'You don't sound too happy about it.'

'It would be fine if the other students weren't on my back all the time. I heard someone whispering "Orc" when I was coming out of my rhetoric lecture. I'd have chopped his head off except then they'd throw me out. Also they don't let me take my axe into class.'

Makri lights up another thazis stick and sets up the opposing forces on the board, the front rank being, from left to right, Foot Soldiers of the Hoplite variety, Archers, then Trolls. The back rank comprises Elephants, Heavy Mounted Knights and Light Mounted Lancers. Each player has in their side a Siege Tower, a Healer, a Harper, a Sorcerer, a Hero and a Plague Carrier. At the very back of the board is the Castle, the object of the game being to defend your own Castle and storm your opponent's.

'Kerk was hanging around outside your door earlier,' Makri tells me.

Kerk is an informant of mine. Fairly useless generally, and a hopeless dwa addict.

'Must have some information for me. He wouldn't come in if he heard I was with a client. I'll look him up tomorrow.'

I open a bottle of beer, pour us out a little klee, draw deeply on my thazis and make my standard opening, sending my Foot Soldiers up the flanks. Makri responds, as she generally does, by sending out her Mounted Lancers to harry them but I notice that she is also surreptitiously preparing to bring her Plague Carrier up the board early. I advance my Archers to support my

Foot Soldiers and make sure my Sorcerer and my Healer are ready to react.

Makri, generally an impetuous player, tries to force an early engagement by suddenly sending out the rest of her Heavy Cavalry, followed by her Elephants. I withdraw slightly and, in a new variation, send my Harper, protected by my Hero, to play to the Elephants. The Harper's music has the power of entrancement and it sends Makri's Elephants to sleep. She can only watch in frustration as my Trolls advance among the immobile beasts and finish them off.

My solid phalanx of Hoplites and Archers is meanwhile holding off her cavalry and I start to send my Siege Tower lumbering up the board. Makri's cavalry are causing casualties among my Hoplites but I've already got my Healer on hand to alleviate the situation. My Sorcerer is meanwhile holding her Hero at bay.

Due to her imprudent attack Makri's Sorcerer is out of position and when battle is thickest in the centre I am able to send my Hero up the right flank with a horde of Elephants and I start to break through. My forces have an awkward moment when Makri suddenly and unexpectedly backtracks with her Plague Carrier and I lose a few Elephants to the plague before my Hero engages the Plague Carrier and puts him to flight. Meanwhile my own Plague Carrier is sneaking up the left flank, weakening Makri's forces. Suddenly I break through on both sides. My Trolls and Heavy Mounted Knights surround and kill her Sorcerer and her Hero. My Hoplites break her cavalry in two and march up the board, followed by my Siege Tower. She tries to muster her forces but her last resistance is broken when my

Plague Carrier kills her Harper before getting in amongst her Trolls and decimating them. Soon I'm swarming over her forces and I move my Siege Tower right up to her Castle.

In niarit it's possible to come back from a poor position but not when playing against a master like me. Makri's remaining forces are hemmed in and gradually whittled down as I prepare my final assault. My Hero leads a horde of infantry up the Siege Tower and into her Castle. Victory to Thraxas.

'Damn,' says Makri, and looks extremely annoyed. She's not a good loser. Neither am I. Fortunately I always win.

'I'll beat you next time,' states Makri.

'No way. I'm still number one chariot around here.'

Makri grins, drinks the rest of her klee in a gulp and departs to her room along the corridor. I struggle into my bedroom, blow out the candle and settle down to sleep. My slumbers are badly interrupted when Hanama, deadliest member of the extremely deadly Assassins Guild, pricks my throat with her dagger. It's a poor way for a man to be woken up after a hard day's work.

CHAPTER
EIGHT

A night candle casts the merest glimmer of light in my room. Barely enough to illuminate the knife at my throat, or the figure of the Assassin looming over me. I'm pinned to my bed, unable to move. A bad awakening indeed. I've encountered Hanama before. She's number three in the Assassins Guild, a ruthless killer. And yet, as my senses clear, I realise I'm not about to be immediately assassinated. If I was I'd be dead already. The Assassins don't worry about formalities like waking up their victims.

'Where is it?' she hisses.

'What?' I croak in reply.

'The Red Elvish Cloth,' says Hanama, plunging me into further confusion.

'What are you talking about?'

She presses the knife a fraction further.

'Hand it over or die,' says Hanama, her eyes as cold as an Orc's heart.

The door to the next room swings open. Light from a lantern floods in. There stands Makri, sword in hand.

'Let him go,' she snarls.

Hanama laughs, a thin, humourless Assassin's laugh.

'Nice bikini,' she says, mockingly, and in one swift movement draws a short sword and drops into a fighting crouch. Hanama's small, thin figure is exaggerated by her featureless black clothes, making her appear almost childlike. I wonder if Makri realises how deadly she is. I ready myself to spring to her aid. Suddenly the outside door crashes open. Men pound into the office and on into my inner room. Makri and Hanama whirl round to face the intruders. I leap from the bed and grab my sword. There's no time to think and little room to move as a horde of savage sword-wielding thugs threaten to sweep us away by sheer force of numbers. A massive man waves an equally massive scimitar at me. I avoid it nimbly and stick my knife into his heart. My next assailant slams a hatchet towards my head. I dodge the blow, kick him in the knee and slash my knife through his throat. I'm good at this sort of thing. So are Makri and Hanama. We drive our attackers back into the next room, then Makri leaps after them impetuously, followed by Hanama and me.

In the larger space of my office we find ourselves at a disadvantage. More attackers are pouring in from outside and they start to encircle us. There's little time to think, though I get a brief glimpse of Makri scything two men down with one blow and flying over a low slash aimed by another to smash her boot into his face. I parry another blow but before I can counter-thrust my senses start going haywire. I detect magic, powerful magic, very close. I gain an impression of a large, cloaked figure in the doorway, one arm raised, before there's a violent flash and I'm thrown back against the wall along with Makri and Hanama. The three of us lie there, gasping and bleeding. I don't know what the spell was but it was pretty effective.

'Kill them,' says the Sorcerer, entering the room.

Suddenly Gurd, roused by the commotion, hurtles into the office with his axe above his head. Two men fall dead before they can scream. I drag myself to my feet as Gurd disappears into a maelstrom of blades and bodies. The interruption allows Makri and Hanama the few seconds they need to recover. A knife flashes out of Hanama's palm, transfixing one man, while she deftly stabs another in the back. Makri hacks her way through to Gurd. I do likewise. Our savage attack begins to carry the day and our attackers start to crumble. One more push should do it. My senses go haywire again and I realise we're in for another sorcerous attack. Damn all Sorcerers.

It's interrupted by the shrill screech of whistles in the alley below. The Civil Guard has arrived. There's confusion as our attackers fight their way down the stairs to make their escape. I don't bother to pursue them. I can hardly stand upright. The exertion of the battle and the effects of the spell have really drained me. Also, I have a hangover.

'What was that about?' demands Gurd, as Civil Guards pile into the room.

I shake my head numbly. I don't know. I look round to check on my companions. Makri is fine, calmly wiping blood from her swords on to the clothes of one of our many dead opponents. Of Hanama there is no sign. She's slipped out in the confusion.

'What was that about?' echoes Captain Rallee.

'No idea,' I pant. 'But I'm sure pleased to see you.'

'We had them beat anyway,' says Makri, dismissively.

Makri fights with a sword in each hand, or a sword in

one and an axe in the other. It's an unusual technique, almost unknown in Turai, and her mastery of the skill makes her pretty much invulnerable against your run-of-the-mill street fighter.

'Look, Captain,' cries one of the Guardsmen, holding up the arm of one of the bodies and pointing to a tattoo. The Captain crosses over to examine it. Two clasped hands.

'Society of Friends,' he says. 'What have you done to offend them, Thraxas? You owe them money as well?'

I shake my head. I had no idea I'd offended the Society of Friends. I try to avoid offending large criminal organisations.

Considering there are nine dead bodies in my room the Civil Guards make surprisingly little fuss. The attackers' tattoos confirm them all as members of the Society of Friends, and the Society cuts little ice down here in Brotherhood territory. The Civil Guard isn't going to waste too much time on the matter, especially as I'm a Private Investigator. Captain Rallee observes that, whatever the reason for the attack, I probably deserved it.

Gurd is distressed at the damage to the room, but reasonably jovial about the whole affair. He hasn't had a good fight for a long time.

'Who was that woman?'

'Hanama. A high-up member of the Assassins Guild.'

Makri's eyes widen. 'There's an Assassins Guild? I never knew they were so organised.'

'Well it's not an official guild. They don't go to meetings with other guilds or send representatives to the Senate. But they exist all right. And a bunch of very deadly killers they are too. They're behind most of the political murders here, and they'll work for anyone who pays them.'

'But she wasn't trying to assassinate you, was she?'

I shake my head. 'She seemed to think I had some Red Elvish Cloth.'

'Huh?'

I shake my head. I can't make it out either. 'The consignment that went missing on its way to Turai,' I explain. 'But what it's got to do with the Assassins, or why Hanama thinks I've got it, is a mystery.'

A municipal cart rolls up outside and some government workers start carrying the bodies out. Tholius, Prefect in charge of Twelve Seas, doesn't spent a lot of the King's money on keeping the place tidy but he does at least provide a service for mopping up corpses.

'What is this Cloth?' asks Makri, as I pour myself a beer to calm myself after the fight.

'The most valuable substance in the west. Worth more than gold or dwa because it's completely impenetrable to sorcery. It's extremely rare and the Elves guard it pretty closely. They make it from the roots of some bush which only flowers every ten years. Or maybe twenty. I can't exactly remember, but it's rare. It's illegal for anyone but the King to own it here. He's got a room lined with it at the Palace where he discusses state secrets with his advisers. Because it forms a total magic-proof barrier it's the only place that's completely safe from prying Sorcerers, so he can be sure that enemy Orcish Sorcerers aren't eavesdropping in wartime for instance. The Orcs don't have any of this stuff, which gives us an advantage. Plenty of people would like to get their hands on some.'

'Were the Society of Friends after the same thing?'

'It's possible. I can't think why else they'd be here. How did word get around that I've got the Red Elvish Cloth? It's got nothing to do with me. It's not even in the city.'

'How do you know?'

'Because the Elves mark all their cloth when it's in transit. A sort of magical signal, so any Sorcerer can locate it. After it reaches our King, an Elvish Sorcerer removes the mark, making it undetectable, but before that's done, Palace Sorcerers could locate it with their searching spells, and I know they've been scanning the city.'

'Maybe whoever stole it removed the mark,' suggests Makri.

'Unlikely. Elvish magic markings are practically impossible to erase. Usually one of their own Sorcerers does it for the King. I wish I knew how I'd become involved in all this. I'd better learn a more powerful locking spell for my door. It didn't take Hanama long to get through it.'

'I like her,' says Makri.

'What d'you mean, you like her? She was holding a knife at my throat.'

'Well apart from that. But she was a good fighter. I always like good fighters.'

'You'll be a fine philosopher, Makri.'

I sleep soundly for what's left of the night. Crisis or no crisis, I'm a man who needs his sleep.

CHAPTER
NINE

I look suspiciously at the coin in my hand. An Elvish double unicorn. Very rare. Very valuable.

'We will pay you another one if you find it.'

I look suspiciously at my visitors. Elves are very well regarded in Turai – fine upstanding race, good warriors, excellent poets, beautiful singers, kind to trees, at one with nature and so on – but I have my reservations. In my line of trade I've seen some evidence of Elvish misbehaviour that most people haven't. Okay, I've never come across an Elf who was a vicious killer like some Humans I've known but I've certainly encountered a few with distinctly criminal tendencies. What's more, in my business a visit from an Elf usually means trouble, because if they have any sort of minor problem then their Ambassador sorts it out for them, with plenty of help from our authorities, who always like to keep on their good side.

Yet here are two young Elves, green-clad, tall, fair and golden-eyed, and they want to hire me. Hire me to find the Red Elvish Cloth. The substance is plaguing me. I've already explained my involvement in the whole affair is accidental.

'If you heard a rumour I have it, it's just that, a rumour. I don't know how it got started but I've no idea where the Cloth is.'

'We have heard no such rumours,' states Callis-ar-Del, the older of the two. 'We have come here because our cousin, Vas-ar-Methet, loyal adviser to Lord Kalith-ar-Yil, who sent the Cloth, recommended you to us as a clever and trustworthy man.'

I enjoy being called a clever and trustworthy man. I look on the young Elves with more sympathy. More importantly, the name of Vas-ar-Methet takes me back. One of the very few Elves I've ever been really friendly with, he came up from the Southern Islands with an Elvish battalion in the last Orc Wars. After the western forces took a beating we ended up sharing a ditch together along with Gurd, ingloriously if prudently hiding from a large Orcish dragon patrol scouting the area. We hid for three days before fighting our way back to safety. Sneaking back to safety might be more accurate actually, but we did have to cut our way through a band of Orcish warriors before we reached the city. It's one of our favourite wartime stories. I relate it at least once a week in the bar downstairs.

'How is Vas these days?'

'He is well. His tree of life grows strong with the sky.'

I don't exactly know what that means but decide not to pursue it.

'Before we left the Islands he instructed us to come to you if we found ourselves unable to make progress.'

The Elves have been sent from the Southern Islands by their Elf Lord to locate the missing Cloth but they have made no progress. So here they are. They've been to their Ambassador, seen our Consul, been to Palace Security, consulted the Civil Guard and asked around at various Investigating Sorcerers uptown, all to no effect. Which brings them to Twelve Seas – rotting fish heads, stinking sewers, cheap detective. Welcome to the big city.

I shrug. Since I'm already involved in this affair, someone might as well pay me now I've been sacked by the Princess. I agree to take the case. The Elves, Callis and his companion Jaris-ar-Miat, tell me what they know, which isn't much. Their Elf Lord, Kalith-ar-Yil, sent up the Cloth on a ship bound for Turai, but it had to put in south of Mattesh because of storm damage. Rather than wait for repairs to be completed the Cloth was loaded on to a wagon train and sent up to the city. Somewhere along the way the escort was murdered and the Cloth disappeared. And that's about it. Callis and Jaris don't seem to have learned anything since being sent to investigate, but then they're not professionals.

I stare again at the double unicorn in my hand. Very valuable indeed. And another one to follow if I locate the Red Elvish Cloth. That would go a long way towards paying off the Brotherhood. Then there's the reward for the Cloth offered by the Consul. Things might be looking up. I might even earn enough to get out of Twelve Seas. The Elves prepare to leave. A very well-mannered pair. They haven't wrinkled their noses at the state of my rooms.

Makri appears, failing to knock as usual. She is taken aback and gawps dumbly at the Elves, who stare back at her. Their manners let them down. They can sense her Orcish blood and it requires little insight to see they don't like it at all. They edge away from her uncomfortably. A look of annoyance flickers over Makri's face.

'Well?' she demands, aggressively.

The Elves nod to me and hurry out. I ask Makri what she wants.

'Nothing. I've got work to do,' she says with what she probably imagines is dignity, and storms out, banging the door behind her.

I'm annoyed. I don't like to see Makri upset, but before I can pursue her Pontifex Derlex appears at my door. I try to look like a man who woke up in time for morning prayers. The Pontifex expresses concern for the attack last night.

'I'm fine,' I assure him. 'Me and Makri fought them off.'

Derlex suppresses a grunt. His concern for my welfare doesn't extend to Makri. With her Orcish blood, chainmail bikini and sword-wielding abilities, Makri is about one step up from a demon from the underworld in the eyes of the Church.

'I am gravely concerned at the increase in crime in the Twelve Seas,' says the Pontifex, fingering his sacred beads. 'As is Bishop Gzekius.'

I grunt. 'I doubt Bishop Gzekius will lose much sleep over me, Pontifex.'

Derlex looks pained. 'The Bishop is concerned with the welfare of every one of his flock,' he says. He keeps a straight face, which is more than most people could do when attributing Bishop Gzekius with any sort of charitable feelings. The good Bishop Gzekius, whose pastoral responsibilities include Twelve Seas and the rest of Turai's miserable dockland slums, is an ambitious schemer with his eyes on the Archbishopric. He's far too busy striving for power and influence among the city's aristocracy to worry about the poor of Twelve Seas, or anywhere else.

'Why did the gang attack you?'

I profess not to know, and usher Derlex out after again promising to attend his church. I'm finding this concern for my health a little hard to take, particularly before breakfast.

My breakfast is a cheerless affair, eaten under the frosty gaze of Makri who is currently as angry as an Orc with a toothache. She slams my plate down on my table and refuses to speak.

'Don't you think you're being a bit over-sensitive?' I venture, as she passes with a mop in her hands.

'I don't know what you're talking about,' she snaps, brandishing the mop in a quite dangerous manner. 'I'm as happy as an Elf in a tree.'

She mops under a chair, knocks it over, and stamps on the remains.

Customers arrive for an early drink, ending our discussion. I curse the delicate sensitivities of my axe-wielding friend and prepare for a day's investigating. I go down to the local Civil Guard station to see if Guardsman Jevox can throw any light on things. I once used my influence to protect Jevox's father from the Brotherhood when they were threatening his livelihood as a book-maker at the Stadium Superbius, which makes Jevox rather more helpful to me than your average Civil Guardsman.

'Any leads on the theft of the Red Elvish Cloth?'

Jevox is surprised at my question. 'You working on that?'

I look vacant and he doesn't press the point. Jevox has heard about the fight at my house with the Society of Friends, but he can't throw any light on why they or anybody else should have thought I had the Cloth. He does tell me that the Society is rumoured to have been connected to the hijacking, though there's nothing definite.

'Are you saying they don't have it any more?'

'Possibly.'

I ask him to let me know if the Guard makes any progress, particularly on the name of the Sorcerer who might be working with the Society, and Jevox agrees. He asks me how I got mixed up in it.

Naturally I decline to explain. 'What's the reward?'

'Just went up to five hundred gurans.'

A nice figure to a man in urgent need of money. Tholius, Prefect of Twelve Seas, arrives unexpectedly and throws me out. Tholius doesn't like me. Prefects never do. Any time I solve something it makes them feel inadequate.

Outside the Civil Guard station some young kid from the Koolu Kings, the local street gang, shouts a disparaging remark about fat men who always gamble on the wrong chariots. I scoop up a stone and hurl it at him in one smooth movement. It hits him on the nose and he bursts into tears.

'Never mock a trained soldier, brat.'

Palax and Kaby are busking beside the harbour. Both are dressed in their usual bizarre assortment of shabby but colourful clothes. They augment their outfits with many strings of beads and great numbers of earrings. Each of them wears a metal stud piercing their left eyebrow (among other parts of their anatomies) and they dye their hair in colours bright enough to get any normal citizen attacked in the street, though as travelling entertainers they have some licence in this sort of thing. Their horse-drawn caravan is parked on a patch of waste ground behind Gurd's tavern. I was shocked the first time I saw them, and recommended that Gurd ran them off the land, but I'm used to them now. They're actually a nice young couple and we're quite friendly. It's beyond me why they have to look so strange though. I mean, pierced noses and eyebrows? Ridiculous. I listen to them play for a minute, and drop a coin into their cup.

It's time to visit the Mermaid, one of Twelve Seas' least pleasant taverns, which is saying something. More youths from the Koolu Kings jeer at me as I pass. Everyone in Twelve Seas knows me, but I wouldn't claim to be popular. The prostitutes and dwa dealers ignore me as I pick my way over the filth strewn over the street.

Kerk can usually be found around here. As a dwa dealer he often learns interesting facts in the way of his business. Unfortunately for him, he consumes rather too much of his own product, and is therefore generally in need of money. I find him outside the tavern, leaning unsteadily against the wall. He's tall and dark but his once handsome features are sunken and undernourished and his large eyes are dull and vacant. From his eyes I think he may have a trace of Elvish blood, which wouldn't be so strange. Elvish visitors to our city are not above dallying with our whores, whatever their professions of moral superiority.

I ask him if he knows anything about the Cloth.

'Choirs of Angels,' he mutters, staring at the floor. I don't know what that means. I presume he's in the grip of some powerful hallucination. Kerk's been getting worse recently. I'm surprised he manages to keep his business going.

'Red Elvish Cloth,' I repeat.

He focuses on me with some difficulty.

'Thraxas. You're in trouble.'

'I know that already. I just don't know why.'

'You robbed Attilan.'

'No I didn't.'

'That's what people say.'

'Well what about it?' I demand.

'Attilan was trying to get his hands on the Elvish Cloth for Nioj. Some people think he already had it when you killed him.'

'I didn't kill him. Or rob him. Anyway, how could Attilan have had the Cloth? It isn't in the city.'

Kerk shrugs. 'Don't know. Maybe Glixius Dragon Killer's behind it all.'

'Who the hell is Glixius Dragon Killer?' I demand.

Kerk looks at me. 'Don't you know anything? You're not much of an Investigator, Thraxas. Surprised you've stayed alive so long. Glixius Dragon Killer is the rogue Sorcerer who hijacked the stuff in the first place. He's been working with the Society.'

Kerk holds out his hand. I press a coin into it.

'Choirs of Angels,' he mumbles again. He dribbles, slides down the wall and passes out. I must find some informers who are not the scum of the earth. At least I now know why my name became connected with the Cloth. Attilan was after it and I had the misfortune to be arrested for his murder. No wonder people thought I'd robbed him.

I stare with distaste at Kerk's unconscious figure. I doubt I'm the only person he sells information to. If he's been spreading what he knows it's no surprise that various other people might think I have the cloth.

It's hot. I want to go home and drink beer. However, with the Assassins Guild and the Society of Friends both out to get me, and two Elves waiting to pay me handsomely, I have an incentive to start work. I need to talk to Captain Rallee but it takes a while to find him. He had a cushy desk job at the Abode of Justice up till last year, which he didn't mind at all, but then he fell out of favour when the wheels of internal Palace politics moved against him. Deputy Consul Rittius replaced him with his own man, and the Captain is therefore once more pounding the streets. Which does at least give me something in common with the good Captain, because Deputy Consul Rittius, the second most important government official in Turai, hates me as well.

I find the Captain staring morosely at a few dead bodies on the outskirts of Kushni.

'What happened?'

'Same as usual,' he grunts in reply. 'Brotherhood and Society fighting over territory for the dwa trade. It's getting out of hand, Thraxas. Half the city's caught up in it.'

We watch as city employees load corpses into wagons and drive them off. I don't bother asking the Captain if he's planning to arrest anyone. The drug barons of the Society of Friends and the Brotherhood have too much protection in this city for the Civil Guard to touch them. As for their lesser minions, there's so many of them it hardly makes any difference how many he throws in jail.

'Just trying to keep the lid on things till I retire,' sighs the Captain. 'And now the elections are about to start. More chaos.'

He shakes his head, and asks me what I want. I explain my situation to him, without mentioning the Elves. He nods.

'We heard a rumour that Nioj was interested in the Cloth. The Elves don't like selling to them. They get annoyed when the fundamentalist Niojan clerics denounce them as demons from hell. Don't think the Niojans were involved in the hijacking though. We've obtained information as to who was responsible.'

'Yeah, I know, Glixius Dragon Killer,' I say, disappointing the Captain. 'I've met him already. Any leads on where the stuff is?'

'No,' replies the Captain. 'But I reckon it's long gone. Probably never reached Turai at all.'

I ask him if the Guards are any closer to finding Attilan's killer.

Captain Rallee sneers. 'We reckon you make a pretty good suspect, Thraxas.'

'Come on, you know I didn't kill him.'

'Maybe. But that might not stop us charging you anyway. If no one better comes along. Rittius would be delighted to see you in a prison galley. And he's going to have to charge someone. The Niojan Ambassador is raising hell.'

'Don't you have any real leads?' I ask him.

'You expect a lot, Thraxas. Information from me, but you won't say what your involvement is. Why should I help you?'

'I once pulled you out from under the wheels of an Orc chariot?'

'That was a long time ago. I've done you enough favours since then. You got yourself mixed up in this, and now the Society's on your tail. Tough. Come clean with us, Thraxas, and I might be able to help you. Otherwise you're on your own.'

That's as much as I get from the Captain, though he does tell me that an even more powerful form of dwa has appeared in the city, going by the name of Choirs of

Angels. No one knows where it's coming from.

'Kerk seems to like it. Well, Captain, if you refuse to help me, I'll just have to find the Cloth myself. I could do with a fat reward.'

'Well, if we find you were mixed up in its theft, you won't get out of prison to spend your reward. Still, Thraxas, maybe you should look for it. If the Society of Friends think you've got it, your life isn't worth much anyway. Not that it's going to be worth anything at all in two days' time if you don't hand over five hundred gurans to Yubaxas.'

I sneer at him.

'No doubt the Civil Guard will provide me with constant protection if a criminal organisation such as the Brotherhood is out to harm me?'

'Yeah right, Thraxas. Sure we will. Best thing you could do is leave town. Except you can't, because you're still a suspect for Attilan's murder. Looks like you're in a difficult position.'

'Thanks a lot, Captain.'

The heat is becoming oppressive. The sun's rays are trapped between the six-storey slums that line the streets. It's illegal to build above four storeys in Turai. Too dangerous. The property developers bribe the Prefects and the Prefects pass on some money to the Praetors' officials and then no one minds that it's dangerous any more. Stals, the small black birds which infest parts of the city, sit miserably on the rooftops, lacking the energy to scavenge for scraps. I'm sweating like a pig, the whores look tired and the streets stink. It's a bad day. I might as well visit the Assassins.

CHAPTER
TEN

Kushni is the most disreputable area of a city which has more than its fair share of disreputable quarters. The narrow, filthy streets are comprised of brothels, gambling dens, dwa joints and dubious taverns. The streets are full of pimps, prostitutes, derelicts, junkies and thieves. It is perverse of the Assassins to have their headquarters there. Not that they're in any danger of being robbed or assaulted by any of Kushni's low-life habitués. No one would be so stupid.

'I'm surprised at you visiting us,' says the black-hooded woman sitting opposite me. 'Our informants didn't say you were possessed of great intelligence, but neither did they tell us you were a fool.'

I'm sitting in a plain room without decoration of any sort talking to Hanama, Master Assassin, and I can't say I'm enjoying it. Hanama is number three in the Assassins' chain of command, or so I believe. They don't publish details of their ranks. She's around thirty, I think, though she looks younger, but it's hard to tell as her head and part of her face are generally covered by a black hood. She is small, very pale-skinned, and rather softly spoken.

'It was easy to break the locking spell on your door,'

she murmurs. 'I doubt if your protection spell would hold out against me for long.'

Little does she know I'm not carrying a protection spell. I put the sleep spell into my subconscious before I came out, and I can't manage two spells these days. Could I utter the sleep spell before she made it across the table to kill me? Possibly. Possibly not. I've no intention of finding out.

'I don't expect to need protection. After all, you're mistaken in thinking I have the Red Elvish Cloth. Why did you think I had it?'

No reply.

'Why do the Assassins want it?'

'What makes you think I would answer questions from you?'

'I'm just doing my job. And protecting myself. If you, the Society of Friends and God knows who else believe I've got the Cloth, my life isn't going to be worth much. The best I can expect is a long stay in the King's dungeon. Or rowing one of his triremes.'

She gazes at me silently. This annoys me.

'Perhaps I should report last night's events to the Civil Guard,' I say. 'The Consul and the Praetors tolerate the Assassins because they find them useful. But they wouldn't be very pleased to hear you were trying to get your hands on Red Elvish Cloth reserved for the King.'

'We would not appreciate anyone spreading false rumours about us,' says Hanama, threateningly.

'I'd hate to do anything the Assassins would not appreciate. You know anything about the theft of the Cloth?'

'The Assassins do not indulge in illegal activities.'

'You kill people.'

'No charges have ever been brought against us,' says Hanama, coolly.

'Yeah, sure, I know. Because you're always hired by people rich and important enough to avoid the law. Why are you looking for the Cloth?'

'We aren't.'

'No doubt you're aware the Cloth is valued at thirty thousand gurans?'

Hanama maintains her cool indifference. I get more annoyed.

'You cold-blooded murderers make me sick. Stay well away from me, Hanama. Bother me again and I'll be down on you like a bad spell.'

Hanama rises gracefully to her feet.

'Our interview is over,' she says, slightly less coolly.

I've succeeded in riling her. Good. Just goes to show what a reckless old fool I've become, riling an Assassin in her own den.

'Just one last question. How do you Assassins all keep your skin so pale? Is it make-up, or special training, or what?'

Hanama pulls a bell-rope. Two junior Assassins enter the room and escort me along a corridor to the front door.

'You should brighten the place up a bit,' I suggest. 'Get a few pot plants.'

They refuse to reply. Practising being grim-faced, I expect. Outside, in the dusty road, I shudder. Assassins. Give me the creeps.

CHAPTER
ELEVEN

Walking through the busy outskirts of Twelve Seas I take my usual short cut through Saint Rominius's Way, a narrow alley. Round the first corner I'm confronted by three men with swords at the ready.

'Well?' I demand, drawing my own sword.

They take a few steps towards me.

'Where's the Cloth, Thraxas?' demands one of them.

'No idea.'

They move to encircle me. I bark out the sleep spell. My three assailants instantly fall to the ground. Very satisfying. I'm most pleased. Every time I do that it gives me a warm glow. Makes me feel like my life has not been entirely wasted.

The sleep spell usually lasts for around ten minutes so I have time for a little investigating before I quit the scene. Delving into their pockets, I find nothing of interest, but they're all tattooed with the clasped hands of the Society of Friends.

Behind me someone speaks. I wheel around, and realise I've made somewhat of a blunder in hanging around. The words belong to one of the arcane languages known only to us Sorcerers, and they formed a common countermanding spell. Which means any spell currently used in the area is no longer operational. Which means that three angry members of the Society of Friends are at this moment coming back to consciousness.

I glare at the Sorcerer with disgust. There's no point in me going to all the trouble of learning, storing and using a sleep spell if he's just going to come along and countermand it. Whilst glaring, I notice that, for a Sorcerer, he's pretty damned big. Carries a sharp-looking blade as well. 'You must be the Glixius Dragon Killer everyone's talking about.' He doesn't reply. The three Friends start climbing to their feet, groping for their swords. I run like hell along Saint Rominius's Way.

I'm worried. Not so much by the blades of the three men – I'll take my chances at swordplay against most inhabitants of Turai – but by the Sorcerer. Something in the way he chanted his counterspell makes me feel that he's a powerful man, skilful enough to be carrying one or two more spells. If one of those is a heart attack spell I'm done for. Even a sleep spell would give them the opportunity to finish me off. I was a fool to pawn my spell protection charm. I must have badly needed a beer.

For a man in poor condition I'm making good time, but as I round the next corner I see three more thugs coming towards me. Six armed men and the Sorcerer. I certainly have offended the Society of Friends.

In front of me I spy a wooden manhole cover. The sewerage system of Turai is one of the wonders of the world, so they say, with a tunnel leading all the way from the Palace to the sea. Not for the first time in my crime-fighting career, I find myself in a position to admire it. I whip off the cover and plunge into the tunnels.

The stench is unbearable. Rats scatter in all directions as I stumble my way through the blackness in front of me. I bitterly regret pawning my illuminated staff along with my protection charm. This is a grim, hellish place to be in the dark. Still, having been here before, I know this sewer leads to the harbour, and just before it discharges into the sea there's another manhole cover through which I can make my escape.

Unsure of whether I'm still being pursued or not I halt and listen.

'Try further down,' comes a voice.

Somewhere behind me is a greenish light. The Sorcerer's illuminated staff. I worry again about how many spells he might be carrying. Rogue criminal Sorcerers are rare in Turai, thanks to the Sorcerers Guild, but when they appear I've no real protection against them. I wade on through the filth, ignoring the stink and the squeaking rats, feeling along the wall for the ladder which will tell me when I'm under the exit. I hope there aren't any alligators down here. Rumours abound of alligators living in the city sewers. I don't think I believe them. Even they must have somewhere better to go. There's a whole sandy bay outside, unless the dolphins chase them in here, I suppose. Dolphins aren't fond of alligators, apparently.

I pick up the pace a little, but this is a mistake because almost immediately a man somewhere behind shouts that he can hear me and this cry is followed by the sound of feet splashing quickly through the water. I curse and hurry on but the splashing footsteps draw nearer.

Round the next bend I pause and turn with my sword and dagger at the ready. An ignominious death, I reflect, succumbing to a heart attack spell in the city sewers. Everyone will think I fell in drunk.

The sewer is around four feet wide and just tall enough for me to stand up in. Not a lot of room for fighting. The faintest of glows appear round the corner, followed by the first of my pursuers, groping his way round, a dagger stretched out in front of him. He's dead before he even sees me, his throat cut by my blade with the sort of well-measured stroke I learned in the Army when I was a confident young soldier and we drove the Niojans back from our walls and the Orcs out of our country.

After this it's not so easy. The next two advance more slowly. A little more light now shows, allowing them to see me more clearly. I use my sword and dagger to parry their dual attack and retreat slightly, aware that this is risky. Who knows what I might trip over down here. The combat is grim and silent. The two Society men drive me steadily back, offering no opening for attack. Behind them I can just make out the dim outlines of their companions, and further back is the largely shadowy outline of the Sorcerer, his staff casting an eerie green light over us all.

My assailants are not top-class fighters – gang members rarely are – but in the confined space of the sewer I find it hard to bring my superior sword fighting skills into play. The sewage comes up to my knees, preventing me from manoeuvring, and all the time I'm worried that the Sorcerer will unleash a deadly spell in my direction, although this depends on what he's carrying. Some aggressive spells are hard to direct. In this tunnel he'd be quite likely to hit his own men too.

The fighter on my right grows impatient and makes a sudden lunge, but he's careless and leaves a gap low down in his defence through which I plant the tip of my sword into his thigh. He groans and stumbles backwards. Another man is about to step into his place when the Sorcerer pulls him back.

'Leave him to me,' he commands, and his staff glows brighter.

I've only a fraction of a second in which to act. I draw back my dagger, preparing to hurl it at the Sorcerer's face, and hope that he's not carrying a personal protection spell. Before I can release the weapon, or he can utter his spell, a horrifying shape erupts out of the water. The swordsman closest to me screams and leaps backwards in fear and the Sorcerer's spell is choked off in mid sentence. Attracted by his light, an alligator surfaces from the mire and grips the Sorcerer's leg in its monstrous jaws.

I look on, frozen with horror. The beast is huge and the grip of its jaws must be terrible. I'm sure it's death for the Sorcerer, but he's not a man who is prepared to surrender his life easily. Mere seconds away from being dragged under the stinking water he shouts out a spell and immediately the alligator starts to writhe dementedly, shaking its huge body around in wild agony, all the while holding on to the leg of the unfortunate Sorcerer.

I turn and flee. He must have used a heart attack spell, or something similar. What this will do to an alligator I'm not certain. Kill it eventually, I'm sure, but maybe not before it killed you. Whether the Sorcerer will survive the encounter is anybody's guess. A dreadful fate if he dies, but the thought that the deadly spell was destined for use on me mitigates my sympathy somewhat.

Heart pounding for fear of encountering another monstrous alligator, I find the ladder. I haul my bulky figure up the creaking rungs as quickly as I ever scaled anything in my life. At the top of the shaft I push off the cover and drag myself into the street. All around people stare in astonishment as, filthy, bedraggled, wild-eyed and stinking, I emerge into the sunlit streets of Twelve Seas.

'Sewer inspection,' I mutter to one inquisitive individual who nears me as I struggle on my way.

'What's it like down there?' he calls after me.

'Fine,' I call back. 'Good for a few years yet.'

CHAPTER
TWELVE

I present a desperate figure as I march into Quintessence Street. The stink from my disgusting sewage-encrusted clothes is unbearable and I'm obsessed with the desire to be clean and to wash the terrible experience out of my system. Down a small alleyway is the public baths. I know the manager well but that doesn't mean she's pleased to see me striding in looking like an apparition from hell.

'Need a wash,' I say as I march past her, ignoring her protests and admonitions for me not to go anywhere near her pool in my condition. Bathers scatter like the rats in the sewer as I make my appearance. Mothers grab their small children out of the water in panic as I walk fully clothed into the water. People scream abuse. There are calls for someone to fetch the Civil Guard to protect them from the plague carrier who's just poisoned their bath.

Ignoring them all, I sink under the warm water and roll around, rubbing the filth from my skin and my clothes. As I let the heat take away some of the tension, I feel some gratitude towards the King. He doesn't do much for the miserable poor of Twelve Seas, but at least he built us a good bathing house. Some time later I emerge clean, my clothes in my hands. I wrap my now sadly bedraggled cloak around my frame and march out, still ignoring the abuse poured on me from all directions.

'Thanks. Pay you tomorrow,' I grunt at the manager, Ginixa, who is loudly promising a law suit against me for ruining her business.

Makri gapes as I appear at the Avenging Axe. 'What happened to you?'

'Bad day in the sewers,' I reply, grabbing a thazis stick on the way up to my rooms. I'm still high on shock and fear, and the effects of my using the sleep spell are starting to show. Spell casting is a tiring business. Even without the subsequent pursuit, putting those Society men to sleep in the alleyway would have taken it out of me. The episode in the sewers has completely worn me out. I need to lie down and sleep, but I'm too worked up to relax. I smoke the thazis in three long draws. Makri arrives with a beer, and in between gulps I finish off the last of my klee. The strong spirit burns my throat as it goes down. Probably there are healthier methods of calming down than thazis, beer and klee, but none so quickly effective. By the time I've gone next door and dressed myself in some dry clothes I'm starting to return to my normal jovial self.

'Who was it?' enquires Makri.

'The Society of Friends. With a Sorcerer.'

'They still think you've got the magic Cloth?'

I nod. There's a knock on the outside door. I answer it with a sword in one hand and a knife in the other. Outside is Karlox, the enforcer from the Brotherhood.

'What the hell do you want?'

'We hear you found the Cloth. Go a long way towards paying off your debts—' he begins.

'I don't have the damned Elvish Cloth!' I yell, slamming the door in his face.

'This is preposterous, Makri. Two Elves are paying me to find the stuff, and everyone else thinks I have it already. It's getting confusing. When I smoked that thazis I swear for a moment I started believing it myself. I'll kill that damned Kerk, it's all his fault. He spread the rumour that I stole it from Attilan.'

I notice that Makri is no longer listening. The mention of the Elves has put her in a bad mood. I'm not certain why it's bothering her so much. Makri has experienced plenty of prejudice against her in the city, with customers downstairs always commenting on her Orcish blood. She doesn't like it but it doesn't usually make her unhappy for long. Often forgets it almost right after hitting the customer. What seems to make matters worse is the fact that it involves Elves. I guess Makri, being one third Elvish, and speaking their language, and detesting Orcs quite as much as they do, finds rejection by them particularly galling. I don't bother trying to cheer her up. Karlox's visit has put me in a pretty bad mood myself.

We light up some more thazis. Our mood improves a little.

'I think the Cloth is still in the city.'

Makri points out that only yesterday I said this was impossible.

'I changed my mind. I don't know how, but that Cloth is in Turai. I can sense it.'

'Very astute, Thraxas. Though I suspected as much myself when all these people started trying to kill you.'

I tell Makri about the alligator.

'You're joking. There aren't really alligators in the sewers?'

I assure her there are. A wave of fatigue rolls over my body.

'I'm going to rest. The Society of Friends probably won't risk another open attack on me down here in Brotherhood territory, but if a Sorcerer with a sore leg comes looking for me, tell him I'm not in.'

It's dark when I wake. A few thoughts of sewers and alligators come to mind but I banish them. More important business calls, namely I'm hungry. Really, really hungry. I launch myself downstairs to investigate Tanrose's cooking. It's now late evening, and drinking at the Avenging Axe is in full swing. Gurd is regaling some off-duty Civil Guardsmen with tales of the time he and a group of fellow mercenaries were trapped south of Mattesh and had to fight their way back to Turai through hundreds of miles of unknown terrain and whole armies of ferocious enemies. It's a true story actually, though I have noticed it does tend to grow in the telling.

Makri, chainmail bikini more or less in place, is gathering tankards and scooping up what looks like a fairly handsome tip from a group of sailors just back from the Southern Islands and full of the wonders they saw among the Elves. I head straight for the side of the bar where Tanrose sits selling her wares and cast a greedy eye over her food.

'Evening, Tanrose. I'll have a whole venison pie, a large portion of each vegetable and three slices of your apple pie with cream. No, better make that four slices. Tell you what, just give me the whole pie. And you'd better give me a bowl of beef stew as well. Stick a few yams on the side will you? What's in the pastry? Pork and apple? Give me two of them, and I'll take six pancakes to mop up the sauce. No, make that eight pancakes and four pastries. Any cake? Pomegranate? Good, I'll have a slice to finish with. A large slice. No, larger. Okay, I'll take the whole cake.'

'Had a busy day?' grins Tanrose, piling up a tray.

'Terrible. Couldn't stop for a bite to eat anywhere. Better make that two venison pies. If I don't eat them Gurd'll only finish them off.'

Vast tray of food in hand, I pick up a special 'Happy Guildsman' jumbo-sized tankard of ale at the bar and retreat to a corner to eat. I have a powerful appetite. Satisfying it gives me intense pleasure.

'One whole venison pie feeds a family of four,' comments Makri, passing with a tray.

'Not if I get there first,' I reply, moving on to the pork and apple pastries, one of Tanrose's specialities. By now the beef stew has cooled sufficiently to let me mop it up with my pancakes, and I wash it all down with the rest of my ale, calling Makri over to bring me a second giant 'Happy Guildsman' tankard to accompany my apple pie.

Some time later, pomegranate cake finished to the last crumb, third 'Happy Guildsman' resting invitingly in front of me, I reflect that life is not so bad. Okay, you might get chased around sewers by the Society of Friends, but there's always Tanrose's cooking and Gurd's ale. Make a man glad to be alive. Makri appears beside me during her break. She makes a few snide comments about my appetite, but I wave them away benevolently.

'You have to stay slim, Makri. You need a good shape

under that bikini to earn tips from sailors. Me, I need something more substantial. You can't solve crimes and face dangerous criminals with only a few morsels inside you. When people see me coming they know they've got a problem on their hands.'

Makri grins. As usual she's carrying a purse on a long string over her shoulder for holding her tips, though I notice that today she has a new one, slightly larger than normal.

'Tips increasing?'

Makri shakes her head. 'Same as ever. I'm using this to carry round some other money I've been collecting. Don't want to risk leaving it in my room.'

'What money?'

'Contributions to the fund.'

'Pardon?'

'You know. The fund for raising money to buy a Royal Charter for the Association of Gentlewomen.'

This is the first I've heard of any fund, although I did know that the Association of Gentlewomen was applying for a Royal Charter, without which they cannot be recognised as an accredited Turanian guild, and take their place on the Council as a member of the Revered Federation of Guilds, and send an observer to the Senate.

'I didn't know you were that involved, Makri. How much have you raised?'

She snorts. 'Only a few gurans. When it comes to the Association of Gentlewomen people round here are meaner than a Pontifex. Gurd won't let me collect in here but I've been going round the local shops. I wouldn't say your average Twelve Seas shopkeeper was keen to contribute. I have a few donations from local women though. Ginixa at the public baths gave me five gurans.'

'If she sues me for ruining her business she might be able to afford a lot more. How much does the A.G. need for the Charter?'

'Twenty thousand.'

'How much have they got?'

Makri doesn't really know. She's only collecting money, and is not involved in the organisation in any major way. She thinks they still have a long way to go.

'And paying for the Charter is only one part of what we need. Before you even make the application, there's the large fee to the Revered Federation of Guilds to process the papers. And all the way along the line there's people to be paid and palms to be greased – the Praetor for Guild Affairs, the Deputy Consul, Palace officials and who knows who else. Apparently it's standard practice for the Consul's Secretary to demand a ten-thousand-guran bribe before he lets an application go through.'

'That's going to add up to a lot of money.'

'It does. And we're going to need twice as much in bribe money because of the opposition from the True Church and all the other people who don't want to see the Association of Gentlewomen make any advance. I heard the figure of fifty thousand mentioned. There aren't many wealthy women in Turai. Even the ones that do run their own businesses have a hard time surviving because the guilds won't admit them. Well, if they won't let us in to the Bakers, Innkeepers, Transport or other Guilds, they're going to have to face us on the Revered Federation Council when the Association of Gentlewomen gets its Charter.'

'Who do you give the money to?'

'Minarixa the Baker. She's the local organiser. Care to make a contribution?'

'What will the Association of Gentlewomen do for me?'

'Get me off your back.'

'Yes, well, maybe later, Makri.'

'Why not now?'

I look around anxiously. 'The place is full of Barbarians and dock workers. If they see me giving money to the Association of Gentlewomen they'll ridicule me half to death.'

Makri sneers. I will give her some money later. Not right now though, not in public. I have an image to maintain.

'You should have asked the Princess, Makri. She must have a lot of money.'

'She hasn't.'

'How do you know?'

'Because I heard at last night's meeting that Lisutaris, Mistress of the Sky, already asked Du-Akai for some help.'

'Lisutaris, Mistress of the Sky? She's pretty senior in the Sorcerers Guild. Works at the Palace too. Is she involved in your group?'

Makri nods. 'All sorts of women are. But the Princess couldn't make a donation. The King controls her money. And they don't get on very well.'

'I'm not surprised, if she lies to the King the same way she lied to me. I still wish I knew why she sent me to find that spell. Why would a Princess want to put a dragon to sleep? It's not like it's guarding anything. No reason to bother with it that I can see. Unless . . .'

I break off, and stare into space.

'Sudden Investigator's intuition?' says Makri, slightly sarcastically.

'That's right. You might want to put a dragon to sleep to make it easier to kill.'

'Why would Princess Du-Akai want to do that? It's a present to her father. They don't get on that badly.'

'I've been wondering how all this fits together, Makri. In my experience, when various troubles descend on me, they generally turn out to be connected in some way or other. No one knows how the Red Elvish Cloth was brought into the city. No one knows where it is now. And if the rumours of the Orcs buying it are right, no one knows how it's going to be transported to them. Well, what if it was put inside something that was very secure, which was going back to them eventually?'

'You mean inside the dragon?'

'Why not?'

'How the hell would you stuff a roll of Red Elvish Cloth inside a dragon?'

'I don't know. But that Sorcerer who chased me through the sewers is powerful. He might have done it after he hijacked the shipment.'

Makri scoffs. 'Dumbest idea you've ever had, Thraxas.'

'Oh yeah? Well, I trust my intuition. And my intuition tells me that the Red Elvish Cloth is right this minute inside the new dragon at the King's zoo. It's the perfect place – in fact it's the only place, because dragons are well known for disrupting sorcery. If the Cloth was inside that beast, our Palace Sorcerers wouldn't be able to detect it, Elvish marks or not. A very clever notion, Makri, very clever indeed. Hide the Cloth in the dragon, wait till it mates with the King's, then off it goes back to Gzak, taking the Cloth with it.'

Makri considers this. Two Barbarians shout for beer but Makri gestures for them to be quiet. 'So what did Attilan have to do with all this?'

'I think he learned of it somehow and decided he'd intervene. Steal the Cloth for his own country. King Lamachus of Nioj would be very pleased with him if he did. Which would explain what Attilan was doing with a spell for putting a dragon to sleep. A Niojan diplomat might be able to gain access to the zoo when it was closed to the public.'

'Where did he get the spell?'

I admit I don't know. But I'm pretty sure he was killed before he used it. Which means the Cloth should still be inside the dragon, right under the noses of the Palace Sorcerers. Just waiting for me to recover it.

I notice Makri seems even more exposed than usual, and is bulging out of her bikini in a manner guaranteed to make even the most experienced sailor's jaw drop.

'Makri, how old are you?'

'Twenty-one.'

'In which case, unless your unique parentage has produced some very strange effects, your breasts should have stopped growing.'

Makri glances at her chest.

'They have. I took a couple of links out of my bikini to make it a bit smaller. I need to earn more tips, Samanatius the Philosopher is starting a new class and I have to raise the fee.'

If Makri ever does make it to the Imperial University no one will be able to say she doesn't deserve it.

CHAPTER
THIRTEEN

Next morning Derlex, the young Pontifex, arrives at my door, thrusting a collection box under my nose. He's come for a donation to the fund for repairing the tower on the local temple, recently damaged in a fire. I rummage around for a few coins. Always pleased to do my civic duty. Also it might get him off my back. It's making me nervous, the way he's always around these days, asking me how I am, encouraging me to go to church. There must be worse sinners than me for him to worry about. Makri appears and Derlex departs with a frown.

'To hell with him,' sniffs Makri, which I guess is exactly what he's thinking about her.

Makri is reading today's copy of *The Renowned and Truthful Chronicle of All the World's Events.*

'Anything interesting?'

'Another Sarin the Merciless story. Apparently she killed a rich merchant in Mattesh and fled with his money. Fought off three Civil Guards who were after her.'

I scoff at this. 'I bet. These news-sheets, they exaggerate everything.'

'How?'

I explain to Makri that I've tangled with Sarin the Merciless before. 'I ran her out of town about six years ago. She was trying to set up some protection racket. The Transport Guild hired me to get her off their back. Bit of a joke, really. She's no killer, just some petty hoodlum with big ideas. The papers always like to build these people up. It gives them something to write about. If she fetches up in Turai I'll soon show her who's number one chariot around here. Hope she does, I could do with some reward money.'

Makri grins. 'Who's Mirius Eagle Rider?' she asks, glancing again at the news-sheet.

'Sorcerer,' I reply. 'Works for Rittius at Palace Security. One of the most powerful Sorcerers in the city, although not averse to dwa, from what I hear. What's it say about him?'

'He's been murdered.'

I raise my eyebrows. That is news. Mirius Eagle Rider murdered? Mirius was not an obvious candidate for murder. There isn't much to the report. Palace Security have it under wraps for just now. But it does contain one notable fact. Mirius was found by one of his servants this morning with a bolt from a crossbow in his back. Strange. A crossbow is an unusual weapon for a murder. Pretty cumbersome thing to carry around as a concealed weapon. It would have to be concealed because it's illegal to carry one in the city. Too powerful, makes the Civil Guard nervous. Generally they're only used in wartime.

Deputy Consul Rittius isn't going to be pleased at such a senior Sorcerer being killed like that. The thought of the Deputy Consul not being pleased gives me some pleasure, although as a man's death is involved I don't get too carried away. Strange, though, that a Sorcerer like Mirius should have succumbed to any normal weapon, no matter how powerful.

'Dwa'd out of his head, I expect. Probably had an

argument with his dealer. These Palace Sorcerers, they're all degenerate.'

'Everyone in Turai is degenerate,' opines Makri. 'I met people with better manners in the Orcish slave pits.'

With that she goes off to her early shift downstairs, and I head off to visit Jevox at the Guard Station to see if he has any information for me. I stop off at Minarixa's bakery and arrive at the station still wiping crumbs off my face. It's already too hot to be comfortable and I'm perspiring freely as I stroll inside. My sword is uncomfortable at my hip. It's chafing at my skin. I never used to notice that sort of thing when I was a young soldier.

Jevox is on duty at the desk. He's mopping his brow as I arrive. 'Hotter than Orcish hell in here.'

'Damn right it is.' I ask him if he's learned anything.

'That Sorcerer who's been chasing you about, Glixius Dragon Killer. He had a big reputation in the west. Very bad, and very powerful. He was expelled from Samsarina a few years back. Involved in an attempted coup.'

Samsarina is a large, wealthy country some way to the west, one of the strongest of the Human Lands. Glixius Dragon Killer. A name I'd never heard before Kerk mentioned it. It doesn't tell me much. Sorcerers always take on exotic names when they finish their training and don the rainbow cloak. He might be able to kill dragons. He might not. He's of aristocratic birth though. Any man with a name ending in 'ius' belongs to an aristocratic family. It's one of these class distinctions we have, just like anyone with 'ox' or 'ax' in their name is low-born. Like Jevox the Civil Guard. Or Thraxas the Investigator.

'Our Prefect got a report he'd been seen in Mattesh.

Left suddenly after the royal vaults mysteriously emptied themselves of gold.'

I wonder if he survived the alligator attack.

'Who's got the Cloth?' Jevox asks me.

I tell him I don't know. I don't mention my theory that it's inside the dragon.

'You know you're famous now, Thraxas?'

'Huh?'

'Prefect Tholius says you were mentioned in a debate in the Senate. Senator Lodius was denouncing the authorities for their incompetence and he cited you as prime example. Wanted to know why you hadn't been arrested and charged with Attilan's death. He claimed there must be some sort of cover-up going on. Is it true?'

I shake my head. I'm not important enough for anyone to cover up for.

'In that case I reckon the Consul might swear out a warrant for you just to shut Lodius up. He's not going to want Lodius accusing the King and his ministers of incompetence with the elections approaching. Maybe it's time you found yourself a lawyer.'

I'm sweating and thirsty so I visit the large street market that separates Twelve Seas from Pashish and buy a watermelon. When I've got most of it inside me I notice Palax and Kaby, who often busk here during the day. They're sitting on a small patch of waste ground next to a fruit stall, talking to someone. As I wander over to say hello their companion rises to leave and I smile, because he's a giant of a man, completely dwarfing the young buskers. He dwarfs me as well, in height if not in girth. He must be close on seven feet tall, with shoulders and biceps to match. Not a man to tangle with, though from the way Palax and

Kaby are waving and grinning I guess he must be friendly.

'Who was that?' I ask, while accepting a draw on a thazis stick Kaby offers me. The mild narcotic is still technically illegal in Turai but since dwa swept the city the authorities don't bother much about it.

'That was Strongman Brex. We used to work with him in the circus, down in Juval. We played music while he smashed rocks with his bare hands. Sometimes he'd come busking with us. He'd hold us up in the air, one on each palm, while we played. We earned a lot of money like that.'

'What's he doing in Turai? Is the circus in town?'

Palax shakes his head. Strongman Brex has apparently left the circus. He'd had enough of the life and came to Turai looking for proper employment.

'He's already got a job. Pity, he won't be able to busk with us.'

'What's he doing?' I ask, passing the thazis back to Kaby.

'He got a job at the Palace. Working for Princess Du-Akai.'

I blink. 'Princess Du-Akai? What's she want with a strongman?'

'Don't know. But Brex likes it. He gets well paid and he doesn't have to smash rocks with his hands any more.'

I leave them to their busking. People round here don't have much money to spare, and if they try playing up in the better areas of town the Guards chase them away.

Why would the Princess want a strongman? I wonder, as I haul myself up the outside stairs towards my office. Bodyguard? Can't be – Palace Security provides her with bodyguards. Maybe it's only temporary employment.

Maybe she just needs someone strong enough to cut open a dragon.

I reach the top of the steps. I open the door and gape stupidly at my room. It appears to have been torn apart by a whirlwind. Papers, broken glass and smashed furniture lie strewn in an incredible jumble across the floor. The last of my precious kuriya is seeping through the floorboards. I groan, and rescue what I can. I do more than groan when I see my only bottle of klee lying smashed beneath a chair. I was saving that.

'Goddamn those Brotherhood pigs!' I roar, unsheathing my sword.

The noise attracts Makri. 'What's happening?' she says, finding me about to march outside, sword in hand.

'That stinking Brotherhood is trying to put the frighteners on me!' I yell. 'Well, I'm not having it!'

Madder than a mad dragon, I storm back down the outside stairs. Makri, perhaps feeling that a single-handed assault on Brotherhood headquarters is a little ambitious, grabs her swords and hurtles down the steps behind me.

I am practically blinded by fury. Gambling debt or no gambling debt, no one comes into my room and smashes my last bottle of klee. I don't have far to go to vent my wrath. There, coming round the corner, is Karlox and his gang, eight of them. They appear surprised as I confront them and start hurling abuse.

'Try threatening me again and you die, Karlox! Who do you think you're dealing with here?'

Karlox grunts angrily. He's a man of few words, too dumb to know many. He draws his own sword and the Brotherhood men fan out. I am ready to fight. Makri stands at my side. A landus wheels round into the street, kicking up a spray of dust and scattering the beggars. A head appears from the curtained window. It's Yubaxas, local Brotherhood boss. He demands to know what's going on. I inform him that I'm about to administer some punishment to his thugs in retribution for wrecking my room.

Yubaxas actually smiles, something he rarely does. It doesn't suit him. 'We didn't wreck your rooms, Thraxas. Not worth the effort. You know the position already. You have three days to pay up, then we wreck you.'

He motions to Karlox and his cronies. 'Get up to Kushni quick. We're needed.'

The landus departs. The Brotherhood thugs trot after it. I'm left standing alone in the street, deflated.

'So, who did wreck your rooms?' asks Makri.

I shrug. I suppose Yubaxas could have been lying, but I can't see why. I don't imagine he was terrified at the sight of me.

Makri kicks a stone. Trudging back to the Avenging Axe, she is disconsolate. 'I was looking forward to a fight,' she says.

'Well, if I don't come up with the money in three days there'll be plenty of fighting to do.'

Makri looks happier. I feel some relief that Makri, despite her weird predilection for studying philosophy, is a keen enough fighter and a good enough friend to automatically support me in a crisis, even though it's not her affair.

I begin the weary task of putting my rooms in order. I've got no idea who wrecked them, or why. I'm in a terrible mood.

CHAPTER
FOURTEEN

Gurd stumbles into the bar from the street outside clutching the remains of a box of tankards.

'There's a riot outside,' he says, as he starts to barricade the door.

A riot. I see the elections are under way. It's always a difficult time in Turai. With the success of the Populares, or anti-monarchy party, things are getting more tense all the time. When Rittius won the position of Deputy Consul last year it was a sensational victory for the Populares, led by Senator Lodius. The Traditionals, covering the Royal Family, Consul Kalius and most of the Senate, regarded it as the end of civilisation. Civilisation is still here, but if Rittius holds on to his post this year, it might not be soon enough. The Royal Family can no longer sweep aside all opposition, but neither are they weak enough to be easily overthrown. Praetor Cicerius is standing for them against Rittius, trying to regain some of the lost ground for the Traditionals. He's an honest man though not particularly popular. Still, he has a chance of victory. Since he was elevated from Senator to Praetor, many people think he's done a good job, and he has the reputation of not taking bribes, which is almost unheard of in this city. People might support him in his bid for the higher post of Deputy Consul.

I muse on things, while the riot rages. Who killed Attilan? Trying to pin down some sort of lead, I decide to work backwards. Where, for instance, did a Niojan diplomat get an Orcish spell for putting a dragon to sleep? Not the sort of thing you can buy at the local apothecary. Could Attilan have obtained it from one of the Orcish Ambassadors at the Palace? Possibly. But if their Ambassadors are anything like our diplomats, they won't be magicians. Diplomats are always drawn from the oldest, most respectable families and they tend not to practise magic, regarding it as beneath them. Orcs have their class divisions and snobberies, just like us. Also, unless utterly treacherous to their country, they would not let such a vital spell fall into western hands. I doubt Orcish diplomats are capable of such treason.

Who else in Turai might have such a spell? There's always the dragonkeeper. Now there's an Orc who might well have such a spell, and could be bribable. Many Orcs are greedy for gold, another attribute they share with Humans. Sometimes I swear if they weren't so ugly I wouldn't be able to tell the difference. I catch sight of my reflection in the mirror behind the bar. I'm no oil painting myself.

I'd like to ask Pazaz a few questions. My Orcish is very rusty so I recruit Makri, who is a rather unwilling accomplice. She's still in a bad mood and it got worse when she was caught in the riot and had to kick her way through to her afternoon ethics class. The prospect of visiting an Orc appals her. Her hatred for Orcs is such that she protests she may not be able to prevent herself from attacking the dragonkeeper on sight. I extract a promise that she will not kill him without provocation but she flatly refuses to leave her swords at home.

'Talk to an Orc without a sword at the ready? Are you mad?'

'He's here under diplomatic protection, Makri.'

'Well, he'll need it if he tries anything with me,' retorts my young and hot-headed companion, fastening on her blade.

I absolutely refuse to let her bring her axe.

'We're visiting the Palace, for God's sake, Makri, not going into battle. And take that knife out of your boot. It'll be hard enough getting you into the Palace grounds without you looking like an invading army.'

The Orcish diplomats are housed in an Embassy within the Palace walls. They never appear in public for fear of causing unrest. We all hate Orcs here. Fair enough. They all hate us. The dragonkeeper is billeted in a small house in the grounds of the zoo, which are open to the public during the day. It's forbidden to speak to him, but I figure it's worth a try.

Makri is afforded some very strange looks by Guards and officials at the huge Lion Gates that open into the Palace grounds, and when it's learned that we're going to visit the King's zoo there are some unpleasant comments from some of the soldiers on duty.

'Must be missing her dragons,' says one.

'Orc,' sneers another.

Makri scowls but manages to restrain her temper until they require her to hand in her sword. They don't insist on me turning in my weapon, and Makri is livid about the prejudice against her. I pacify her the best I can, which is hardly at all, and we enter the Palace grounds with Makri angrier than a wounded dragon and threatening terrible vengeance on the next person to insult her.

The King's Palace in Turai is one of the wonders of the world. Many larger states than us have far less impressive imperial buildings. Since money started flowing in from the gold mines a few generations back, various Kings and Princes have turned their hands to building an ever more splendid residence for themselves.

Behind the huge Lion Gates, six times the height of a man, is a fabulous den of luxury. The gardens alone are famous throughout the Human Lands, with towering arbours, vast lawns, avenues of trees, banks and beds of flowers, all fed by streams and fountains that were engineered by Afetha-ar-Kyet, the great Elvish garden-maker of a few generations back. The Palace itself is a vast edifice of white marble and silver minarets. The courtyards are paved with pale green and yellow tiles imported from the far west and each wing is roofed with golden slates. The corridors and state rooms are covered with mosaics of gold leaf and coloured stone, and the private quarters were decorated by artists and furnishers drawn from all over the world.

I used to work here. When I was a Senior Investigator for Palace Security I had the run of the place. Now I'm about as welcome as the plague.

The grounds are vast and it takes us some time to reach the zoo. It's hot, and I'm tired. I don't much feel in the mood for seeing Orcs or dragons. I point out a few of the architectural glories which surround us to Makri, but she's in too bad a mood to admire them, even though architecture would be part of the University course. Her bad mood intensifies deeply when the call for Sabam

rings out from a nearby tower and we are obliged to
kneel and pray. I have to practically wrestle her to the
ground. If we failed to make our prayers right here in the
public grounds of the Palace we'd be up on an impiety
charge so quick our feet wouldn't touch the ground.

I have trouble staying awake in the heat and doze off
during the prayers. Makri unceremoniously boots me
awake. I ignore her coarse witticism on my religious
shortcomings and haul myself to my feet. The zoo is now
in sight but as we approach its white walls a fearful
commotion erupts and Guards and civilian officials start
pouring this way and that. We hurry on and reach the
zoo but the entrance is barred to all the people flock-
ing round from every direction. I recognise various
important Palace officials, including Kalius the Consul.
The Niojan Ambassador arrives in a sedan, followed by
another sedan with thick curtains and an odd, alien
crest on the side. The Orcish Ambassadors. One of the
Royal Princes hurries past with his bodyguard. What on
earth is going on?

Behind the Prince comes, of all people, Pontifex
Derlex. I grab the priest's arm and demand to know
what's happening.

'The new dragon's been killed!' he yells. 'It was cut
open during prayers! Princess Du-Akai's been arrested!'

CHAPTER
FIFTEEN

I have no opportunity for further enquiries as Makri, myself and everyone else are summarily evicted from the grounds. We share a landus home with Pontifex Derlex, who is so excited by the whole affair he doesn't seem to mind travelling with Makri, the demon from hell. It's a lot for him to be excited about, I suppose. Derlex is a fairly lowly local priest. He'd never normally be found at the Palace but he had been invited there as the guest of Bishop Gzekius, who was presiding at some religious ceremony for the Royal Family.

The sensational story soon spreads all over Turai. People gather on street corners and bars to speculate over the affair and study the latest reports in the special editions of the news-sheets. It's one of the most serious scandals anyone can remember, and it is bound to have great repercussions. Senator Lodius is already fulminating against corruption in the Royal Family. The Populare candidates in the forthcoming elections are fighting to outdo each other in condemning the decadence and graft that they say is gripping the city. Personally I take little interest in politics, and any enthusiasm I might have for reform is tempered by the fact that Senator Lodius is in reality a nakedly ambitious power-seeker ready to use any means to attain his ends.

Deputy Consul Rittius belongs to his party, which suggests how bad it is.

None of this matters to me right now. What does matter is the sensational events at the King's zoo. The dragon had its belly slit open, not the easiest of things to accomplish, given that a dragon's skin is like armour. Arrested at the scene along with the Princess was Strongman Brex, with an axe over his shoulder. When the Princess was found to be carrying a large quantity of dwa it was presumed that she had somehow drugged the beast before Brex hacked it open. As far as I can learn, no one knows why they did it.

Naturally the Orcs are furious. The King is furious. The population is in uproar. And when you consider that the Niojan Ambassador is still threatening war if the murderer of Attilan is not brought to justice, it might be a good time for the faint-hearted to vacate the city. Senator Lodius is going to exploit this to the utmost, which means the elections will be more violent than usual. We're in for a tough time this summer, unless the Niojans just invade and get it over with.

Makri is hurrying her meal before rushing out to tonight's class. Principles of geometry, I think. She's wrapped in the all-over cloak she's obliged to wear at the Institute to prevent her from panicking the young scholars.

'What are you going to do?' she asks me.

'See if I can find out where the Princess has hidden the Cloth. It hasn't come to light yet, and no one else seems to realise that it was hidden inside the dragon. I might still be able to recover it for the Elves.'

'Aren't you going to help the Princess?'

'Of course not. She isn't paying me, and I don't owe her any favours.' Sometimes Makri just doesn't understand the commercial nature of my business. I don't help people for fun. I do it for money. Anyway, the Princess may well be beyond help. If she's foolish enough to be caught slaying the King's dragon, that's her problem.

Of course, if I keep on looking for the Cloth it might be harder to convince those murderous people who think I already have it to leave me alone. But that's my problem.

This evening, life in the Avenging Axe is in full swing. Mercenaries, dockers, labourers, pilgrims, sailors, local vendors and shop workers drink heartily, washing away their troubles. Young Palax and Kaby arrive and get out their mandolins, flutes and lyres and start entertaining the crowd with some raucous drinking songs, stomping traditional folk dances and a few maudlin ballads for the tavern's lonely hearts. They're good musicians and popular with the crowd, which is just as well really, or they might suffer more than the friendly abuse they already get for that brightly dyed hair and those colourful clothes and pierced ears and noses. Gurd pays them with free drinks. Quite a good scam really. Makes me wish I played an instrument.

Despite all the jollity Gurd is looking as miserable as a Niojan whore and fails to respond when I clap him on the back and ask him if he remembers the time we faced fourteen half-Orcs in the Simlan Desert with only one knife between us and still came out on top. He looks at me gloomily then asks if I'll come and see him tomorrow.

I nod, though it's not something I'm looking forward to. The talk I imagine will be about the cook, Tanrose, with whom Gurd thinks he may be in love. As an old bachelor who's spent most of his life wandering the earth as a mercenary, Gurd finds this very confusing. He can't make his mind up what to do, not wishing to offer her his hand in marriage and then find out that what he thought was love turns out later to be merely an infatuation with her excellent venison pies. He frequently asks my advice on the matter, even though I've pointed out that I have a poor record in affairs of the heart. Still, lending him a sympathetic ear is always a good thing. Makes him more tolerant when I'm late with the rent.

People laugh, dance, gamble, swap stories and talk about the day's scandalous affair. By the light of the oil lanterns Palax and Kaby work up a furious rhythm which has the whole tavern either dancing or stamping their feet. I bang my tankard on the table in time to the beat, and shout for more beer. All in all, it's a fine night in the Avenging Axe; more fun with the poor of Twelve Seas than I ever had with the aristocrats at Palace social functions. I end up hideously drunk, which would be fine but, just as Gurd and Makri are carrying me upstairs, Praetor Cicerius arrives. He is Turai's most famed Advocate and a man of great influence in the city. He informs me that I have to come up to the Palace and interview Princess Du-Akai right away.

It takes me some time to realise what he means, and for a while I keep trying to tell the Praetor it's no good. I've heard the rumours about his wife but I don't do divorce work.

'There are no rumours about my wife,' retorts

Cicerius, who is not the sort of man you can have a laugh and a joke with. He's around fifty, thin, grey-haired, austere, and is famously incorruptible. I invite him to join in an obscene Barbarian drinking song I learned from Gurd. He declines.

'Why don't you sort things out in this city, Praetor?' I demand, suddenly aggressive. 'Everything's going to hell and the government's about as much use as a eunuch in a brothel.'

Colour drains from the Praetor's face. Gurd and Makri abandon me in disgust. The Praetor's two servants pick me up bodily and bundle me outside and into a landus, which Cicerius is allowed to ride at night as part of his senatorial privilege. I begin to enjoy the experience, and start bellowing the drinking song out the window as we ride through the quiet streets of Pashish. Cicerius looks at me with contempt. Let him. I didn't ask him to come visit me.

'No use looking at me like that,' I tell him. 'If the Princess chopped off the dragon's head, it's her fault, not mine. Bad thing to do. Poor dragon.'

I fall asleep, and have only dim memories of being carried into the Palace. The servants are insulting about my weight. I insult them back. I'm not the first man carried drunk into the grounds of the Imperial Palace, though I may well be the heaviest. I'm deposited in some building I don't recognise and the servants start forcing deat down my throat. Deat is a hot herbal drink. Sobers you up. I detest it.

'Gimme a beer,' I say.

'Get him sober,' says Cicerius, not bothering to conceal his loathing and contempt. 'I will bring the

Princess. Though why she insists on seeing him is beyond me.'

I drink some deat, fail to sober up, and start wondering exactly where I am.

'The reception room of the Princess's chambers,' a servant tells me.

'Right,' I grunt. 'I suppose Princesses don't get thrown in the slammer like ordinary people.'

I think of all the times I've been thrown in jail and get slightly maudlin. 'Nobody loves me,' I tell the servant.

Cicerius arrives back with Princess Du-Akai. I greet them genially. The Princess thanks me for coming. She doesn't comment on my drunkenness. Good breeding.

'I am in grave trouble.'

'I bet you are.'

'I need you to help me.'

'Too bad,' I say, again gripped by alcoholic aggression. 'I'm all out of help for clients who lie to me.'

'How dare you speak to the Princess like that,' roars Cicerius, and we start to argue. Princess Du-Akai intervenes. She motions both the servants and the Praetor outside, and draws up a chair next to me.

'Thraxas,' she says, in the most pleasant of voices. 'You are a drunken oaf. Tales of your misdemeanours while working at the Palace do not do you full justice. In the normal course of affairs, I would have nothing whatsoever to do with you. You're so far below me in the social ladder I wouldn't notice if I stepped on you. That woman with the Orcish blood is better bred than you. As well as being a drunk, you're gross, and a glutton, both qualities I despise. You belong in your slum in Twelve Seas, and I'd much rather you were there than here in this room with me. However, I need your help. So sober up, stop playing the fool, and get ready to listen.'

'I seem to be doing a lot of listening already. Why should I help you?'

'For two reasons. Firstly, I shall pay you extremely well. I understand you are badly in need of money. Gambling is another of your bad habits.'

I curse. My gambling debt seems to be the most talked about thing in this city. Even the Royal Family knows about it.

'What's the second reason?'

'If you don't help me, I will ensure that your life in this city is hell on earth. I may be heading for a secure cell in a nunnery but I'm still third in line to the throne, and I have more influence in my little finger than you have in your whole fat body. So listen.'

She holds out a heavy purse. I listen.

SIXTEEN

When I'm finished listening I'm led into the next chamber by a servant. Cicerius is waiting for me. He is no more friendly than before. The fact that the Princess thinks I can help her doesn't make him any keener on me. Cicerius is not known for his affability. Despite his unparalleled reputation for honesty he is commonly regarded as a rather distant and austere man. Senators rarely hobnob with commoners like myself, and Praetors never do, except when they need their votes.

As I enter he is in animated conversation with a younger man whom I recognise as his son, Cerius. The Praetor sees me enter but does not acknowledge my presence so I sit down heavily and wait for him to finish. I'm tired and want to go home and sleep. Damned Princess.

Finally Cicerius turns to me. 'I trust your interview was satisfactory.'

'Very satisfactory,' I brag. 'The Princess knows I'm number one chariot when it comes to investigating so she's decided to put the whole affair in the hands of a man who can get things done. Smart woman, the Princess.'

Cicerius fixes me with a hostile gaze. He is famous for

his oratory and advocacy in the law courts. Part of his considerable armoury while making speeches is his range of facial expression, and the expression he wears when looking at me speaks volumes, rather like a man peering at a rat crawling out of a sewer. No way to behave when he's trying to be elected to a public post, I would've thought, but I suppose he doesn't care too much about my vote.

If I am to help the Princess I'll need Cicerius to open a few doors for me. While we are discussing arrangements, we are interrupted by the arrival of a Captain from Palace Security.

'Praetor Cicerius,' he says, 'I have a warrant here for the arrest of your son, Cerius.'

The Praetor masks his outrage, and demands quite coldly to know the reason why.

'A charge of importing dwa,' says the Captain. He shows Cicerius and Cerius his warrant then puts his hand on Cerius's shoulder. Cicerius is left speechless as his son is led away. It's a cruel stroke and a well-timed one by his rival Rittius. Praetor Cicerius has just lost his family and the election at the same time.

I walk up to him. 'Hire me,' I say. 'I'll help your son.'

Cicerius glares at me with increasing loathing before marching swiftly out of the room.

'Only trying to help,' I say to the servant as he guides me out.

It's around two in the morning when I arrive back at the Avenging Axe. I'm fairly sober, sober enough to avoid stepping on the drunks and desolates who litter the night-time streets, or tripping over the wreckage that's still piled up after the riot. I have a headache. I'm tired. I can't stand any more aggravation. When I reach my room it has again been wrecked.

I stare at the incredible mess with dumb fury. Every piece of furniture has been reduced to matchwood and everything I own is strewn over the floor. Who is behind this? Whoever it is I swear an oath to run them through and dance on their remains.

Makri's a light sleeper. She's woken by my cursing and appears with a sword in her hand. She's naked.

'Shouldn't you get dressed before you challenge intruders?'

'What for? They'd be dead before they noticed I wasn't wearing anything. What's going on?'

'My room's been wrecked again,' I say, needlessly. Makri offers me the use of her couch. I shake my head.

'I wasn't planning on sleeping yet. I'm still working. And I need you to come and speak Orcish. Cicerius has arranged for me to see the dragonkeeper.'

'Now?'

'Has to be. If things get any worse for Cicerius he might not have enough influence to even get me into the zoo.'

'How come?'

'His son just got arrested for dealing dwa. But that's his problem, he doesn't want any help from me. I'm working for the Princess again. I'll explain on the way.'

Makri nods, and departs to get dressed. She loads up with weapons and I don't object. On our way back to the Palace I fill her in with the details.

'Princess Du-Akai claims she's innocent. She admits she was going to cut open the dragon to get the Red Elvish Cloth. Which is why she wanted the sleep spell originally. I asked her if she'd got the spell back but she denied it. That's why she had the dwa, to try drugging the beast. Anyway, someone beat her to it. So when the King and his retinue walked in and found her and Strongman Brex standing beside the dead dragon with an axe and a big bag of dwa it naturally looked suspicious.'

'Naturally. Where did she get the dwa?'

'She stole it from the apartments of her brother Prince Frisen-Akan, though she didn't tell the King that. He doesn't know what a degenerate his oldest son is. I reckon the King might have tried to hush it up about her killing the dragon but Senator Lodius was there on official business. Naturally he started raising a scandal right away.'

'So what are we going to do?'

'Find out who really killed the dragon before the Princess is dragged in front of the special Royal Judiciary and sentenced to life in a nunnery. You see I was right about the Elvish Cloth, Makri, even if no one else realises. It was inside the dragon. Find that and we'll find the killer. Maybe the killer of Attilan as well.'

'Are you hired for that?'

'Not exactly. But Turai badly needs to produce a culprit. Nioj is raising hell about it. Cicerius agreed that a reward would be forthcoming if I cleared the matter up. Praetor Cicerius is a pillar of the establishment, or was till his son was arrested. He's as cold as an Orc's heart but he's also one of the few men in Turai I'd trust. Incidently, he regards me as the scum of the earth. Just his bad luck I'm the only one who can help the Princess. Mind you, I'm not entirely sure the Princess didn't kill

Attilan, or have him killed. She *was* having an affair with him. That's how she learned about the stolen Cloth and Attilan's plan to intercept it for Nioj. Attilan had heard about it from a Niojan agent who was spying on the Orcish Ambassador. The Orcs initiated the whole thing. They hired Glixius Dragon Killer to steal the Cloth and load it into the dragon so they could ship it home later. Who else knew about all this I'm not sure, but it's a safe bet others learned of it. Turai is a hard place to keep a secret, especially in diplomatic circles, with Sorcerers prying everywhere. Anyway Attilan bribed the dragonkeeper to let him have an Orcish spell for putting the dragon to sleep so he could recover the Cloth. Princess Du-Akai decided it would be a good idea if she did it instead, which is why she sent me to recover the box with that phoney story about the love letters. Which is where we came in, more or less. I guess whoever ended up with the spell took the opportunity of the Royal Family all being at their religious ceremony to sneak into the zoo and do the deed. I've no idea who it was though. Not many people have access to the private zoo at that time of day. Diplomats mainly. There again, the Brotherhood and the Society of Friends are quite capable of bribing their way anywhere.'

'How did the Assassins get involved?'

I shrug. That's a loose end I'm far from tying up. Why Hanama wanted the Cloth is a mystery. But it is never easy to interpret the actions or motives of the Assassins. As far as I am aware they never hire out their services for any purpose except murder, but who knows? Maybe they've taken up investigating as a sideline.

'I can't see an Assassin like Hanama wanting to be an Investigator,' says Makri.

'Why not? It's better than rowing a slave galley.'

We're now almost at the Palace. Makri has digested everything I've said, as she always does, being a smart woman, but she does wonder why the Princess wanted the Elvish Cloth in the first place.

'She wouldn't tell me, even in private. Maybe she was acting from patriotic motives, to prevent the Orcs or the Niojans getting it. More likely, knowing our Royal Family, she's got secret gambling debts and needed the money. Probably planned to sell it to the Orcs herself.'

'So who are you finding it for now? The Elves or the Princess?'

'I'm finding the Cloth for the Elves. And I'm clearing the Princess of dragon murder.'

'You'll get confused.'

'Confused? Me? When it comes to multiple investigations I'm sharp as an Elf's ear. Anyway, I need the money.'

The landus enters the Palace gates.

'Time to meet an Orc,' I say to Makri. 'Keep your sword in its sheath, I need to hear what he's got to say.'

SEVENTEEN

Orcs are a little larger than Humans, and slightly stronger. But uglier. They're much given to wearing crude jewellery with motifs of eagles and skulls, and probably originated the nose-, lip- and eyebrow-piercing style with which Kaby and Palax now distress the respectable population of Turai. Craggy-faced with dark, inky-red skin, they generally dress in dark shaggy leather clothes of simple design and wear their hair long. They're usually savage fighters and, despite what Humans say, are not stupid. I know that their diplomats have proved to be shrewd negotiators. It's said in the west that most Orcs do not read, and there is no literature of any sort in any of their nations, but Makri claims this is not true. Nor, she says, is it true that they play no music; nor are they cannibals. She even says she's seen Orcish paintings, though I find this very hard to believe. Makri loathes all Orcs, but refuses to admit that Humans are much more civilised. I know little of their civilisation. The only time I've encountered Orcs has been in battle, and most of the ones I've faced have ended up dead before we had a chance for much conversation. I've never even seen a female Orc, or a child.

As is the case with the Human Lands, Orcs speak their own national dialect as well as the common Orcish tongue. Very few people in the west know any Orcish – it's regarded as very unlucky even to utter a word of it – so Pazaz the dragonkeeper is surprised and disconcerted when Makri addresses him in the common Orcish language. He's naturally suspicious, but as he's been told by his superiors to cooperate with the investigation, and we're bearing a letter from the Praetor himself, he answers our questions.

'He claims not to know anything about the killing,' reports Makri, who is herself finding the conversation very unsettling. The last time she talked to an Orc, she was their slave, and she doesn't enjoy the memory. 'He's upset though. He liked the dragon.'

'He liked it?'

'Used to read it stories at bedtime.'

'Ask him if he sold the sleep spell to anyone but Attilan.'

Pazaz denies that he sold a dragon sleep spell to anyone at all but we tell him we know he's lying. I threaten to inform his Ambassador and he breaks down a little. He admits selling a copy to Attilan, but swears there was no one else.

It's difficult to know if he's telling the truth. I get a feeling with most suspects, but the emotions behind this craggy face are strange and unreadable. I lay some more of my cards on the table and tell him I know all about the plot to export Red Elvish Cloth to Gzak. Now he is really worried. Even though he's under diplomatic protection he'd find himself in an uncomfortable position if the population of Turai learned about it. There's enough bad feeling in the city about Orcs being here at all, without it being known that they've been trying to steal our magical secrets.

Nothing in his answers brings me any closer to learning who killed the dragon, or where the Elvish Cloth might be now. Praetor Cicerius told me that the religious ceremony attended by the Royal Family had lasted no more than half an hour. Whoever came here and killed the dragon must have had good inside information, but in a city as corrupt as Turai good inside information is available to anyone for a price. More interestingly, Cicerius also informed me that the Investigating Sorcerers from Palace Security have been unable to detect the aura of any unusual visitors to the zoo, which makes matters worse for the Princess. Still, with the dragon's disruptive effect on any magical field, it's not absolutely certain that no stranger has been here.

'It can't have been easy for anyone to kill the dragon and remove the Cloth, sleep spell or not. Has no one been around showing any unusual interest in its habits?'

No one has, according to Pazaz. No one talks to him at all, apart from Bishop Gzekius, who's made one or two attempts to convert him to the True Religion. I'm almost moved to sympathy for the Orc. Bishop Gzekius is always trying to put one over on his fellow Bishops. Probably wanted the Orc's soul as a trophy.

It's time to leave. Apart from having my suspicions about Attilan confirmed, I haven't learned much. Lights burn still in the Palace as we're led through the grounds to the gates. Inside I expect everything is in uproar, due to the arrest of the Princess. Times are changing. At one time a Princess would never have been arrested in Turai, no matter the crime. A Praetor's son wouldn't have been arrested either. Now, with Senator Lodius's Populares increasing in power, the upper classes are feeling the pinch. Do them good maybe, having to obey the laws of the land.

I am dead tired. The heat of the night weighs me down. I could happily lie down and sleep where I am. The stress of the day and my tiredness is making my head pound; the prospect of facing my room, once more in ruins, makes it worse. We travel back in silence to Twelve Seas. Makri's thinking about Orcs. She tells me later that Pazaz had seen her fight in the arena, which made her feel even more like killing him.

'The next time I meet an Orc it'll take more than diplomatic protection to keep his head on his shoulders,' she says before lapsing into gloomy silence. Neither of us has any inspiration. The night is oppressively warm and all I want to do is clear a space on my floor and sleep. Which is something I can't yet do, because there at the Avenging Axe, in his blue-edged Praetorian toga, is Cicerius in a landus, with his customary severe expression and a couple of servants looking nervous to find themselves in Twelve Seas in the middle of the night.

I've had my fill of the upper classes. I'm so tired I can't even be bothered to be rude. I just ask Cicerius if he can wait till tomorrow for the progress report on the Princess.

He hasn't come for a progress report. He's come to hire me to get his son off the hook. I fail to stifle a yawn, and lead him inside. I help myself to a flagon of ale from behind the bar and try to concentrate on what Cicerius has to say. I could cope with being Turai's cheapest Investigator but I'm finding it hard being the busiest.

CHAPTER
EIGHTEEN

One thing abut Cicerius, he's a man for plain speaking when necessary. He apologises stiffly for his former brusque refusal of my offer of help, and admits that I am probably the man for the job.

'As you know, my son Cerius Junius has been accused of dealing in dwa.'

One time that might have shocked me. It doesn't any more.

'Deputy Consul Rittius, acting on information, obtained a search warrant this evening. He visited my house while I wasn't there. In the course of his search he found dwa in Cerius's rooms.'

'How much?'

'Two imperial pounds.'

'Right. Too much for personal use. Who's he dealing it to?'

Cicerius looks pained. 'I refuse to believe that my son is a dwa dealer.'

I point out that these days even the most respectable families are finding themselves involved in dwa. Cicerius frowns. His famous eloquence departs him as he considers the prospect of his son ending his days in a prison galley.

'So what do you want me to do?' I ask, drinking some beer.

'Find out the truth. As you know, Rittius and I are bitter rivals and are standing against each other for the post of Deputy Consul. He has leapt at the chance to discredit me. If Rittius defeats me and remains Deputy Consul, great harm will come to the city.'

By which Cicerius means that Lodius's Populares will gain the ascendancy. As a bastion of the Traditionals, Cicerius doesn't like the thought of that at all. Not being interested in politics, I don't much care.

'I'd say you're discredited already.'

'Not quite. Consul Kalius has no wish to see my son ruined. Nor does he wish to see me discredited and the Populares gaining ground. With the political situation in Turai being so volatile these days, it is vital that Senator Lodius does not increase his influence.'

'So the Consul is going to sweep it under the carpet? Then why do you need me?'

'The Consul will not sweep it under the carpet,' retorts Cicerius with asperity. 'All citizens in Turai are subject to the law. But he will see that the case is not brought to court if Cerius names the people he bought the dwa from, and whom it was intended for. That is standard practice.'

True enough. Many small dwa dealers have wormed their way to freedom by selling out their larger partners in crime.

'Unfortunately Cerius absolutely refuses to speak. I cannot understand it. All he has to do to safeguard his reputation, not to mention his family's, is tell the Consul the full story. He refuses.'

Poor Cicerius. You spend all your time being the most respectable politician in Turai then your son goes and gets arrested for drugs. Just goes to show that even the blue-lined Praetorian toga can't guarantee you happiness.

'You're the finest lawyer in Turai, Cicerius. I've heard you tearing people apart in court with your cross-examination. If you can't get anything out of your son, what makes you think I will?'

Cicerius looks pained. The whole episode has obviously come as a terrible shock to him. He admits that his courtroom techniques somehow don't seem suitable for dealing with his son.

'Also I have little experience of these matters. Even in these decadent times I did not imagine that a young man of Cerius's character would become involved in dwa. Furthermore, in the few hours since this happened, I have already invited Tuparius to investigate the matter. Tuparius could learn nothing from my son.'

Tuparius. A high-class Investigator. Works out of Thamlin. I don't like him much but he's not a bad Investigator compared to some of the others that work up there.

'Is he still on the job?'

Cicerius nods. I don't mind too much. Frankly, in a case of dwa dealing I wouldn't expect Tuparius to come up with much. Not enough low-life contacts.

'Even if you can learn nothing directly from Cerius,' continues the Praetor, 'I shall expect you to find out full details of the business, including where the dwa came from and who it was for. Once that information is passed on to the Consul, Cerius will not be brought to court. If he is not brought to court, we may keep it from reaching the ears of the public.'

'Rittius is down on you like a bad spell. He'll make sure it does.'

Cicerius raises one eyebrow slightly. Which means, I imagine, that he still has enough influence around here to hush it up, providing there is no court case.

'How long do I have?'

'It generally takes one week till the preliminary hearing. After that it will be too late.'

I point out that I am already busy, far too busy to be wading into another case.

Cicerius points out that the public scandal will undoubtedly hand the election to Rittius. Which isn't so good for me, I must admit. Even if I don't care about politics, my life would be easier if the Deputy Consul wasn't a man who hated me. If I help Cicerius here, and he wins the election, then the new Deputy Consul would be in my debt. I become slightly more enthusiastic. Maybe I'll get back into the Palace one of these days after all.

Really I'm too busy to take on the case. I think about the money I owe the Brotherhood. I'm not scared of Karlox, but I can't fight them all.

'I'll take the case.'

I pick up my standard retainer and another thirty for expenses, and promise to get on the job first thing in the morning. The Praetor departs. Makri, waiting silently all this time, is of the opinion that I am foolish to take on more work.

'That's three difficult cases at once. You'll end up making a mess of all of them.'

'I need the money. I got two days left to pay off Yubaxas, and who knows if I'll recover the Cloth in time to get paid before the Brotherhood come after me. I'm in no position to turn down employment. And don't bother lecturing me about my gambling, I'm too tired to take it in.'

I clear the junk off my mattress and sleep, but not for long. Kerk wakes me up by kicking my door. He has some information to sell and badly needs his morning dose of dwa. The early interruption to my slumbers puts me in a foul mood.

'Make it quick,' I snap.

'Well you look as happy as a dragon with a headache,' mutters Kerk, and grins stupidly. 'I got some information about Prince Frisen-Akan.'

I frown. I've already had enough of the Royal Family. 'What about him?'

'He's importing dwa.'

I'm almost moved to laughter. That the heir to the throne should be a drug dealer is quite in line with our national character these days.

'What's that got to do with me?'

'He's a friend of Cerius.'

Word has got around quick about this one. I don't bother asking Kerk how he knows about Cerius. He's generally well informed about drug-related matters in Turai.

'And?'

'Cerius was holding on to the dwa for him.'

I frown again. It's going to be difficult clearing young Cerius's name if it involves implicating Prince Frisen-Akan. Hardly the sort of result Cicerius is looking for.

I place a small coin in Kerk's hand. He looks at it with contempt, and demands more.

'Or I won't tell you who else is involved.'

I press another coin in his hand. His hand trembles. He needs his dwa, and quickly.

'Glixius Dragon Killer.'

'That's all I need. You sure?'

'Absolutely. He's overseeing the operation in the city. He's working with the Society of Friends. And the Prince is bankrolling them. They're bringing in Choirs of Angels. Very good. Very strong. And cheap.'

I demand to know how Kerk knows all this.

'Simple,' he says. 'Cerius told me. He can't hold his dwa. Rambles like an old man.'

Kerk laughs, but it costs his broken-down body a great deal of effort. I ask him who's supplying the Choirs of Angels, but Kerk doesn't know. He's becoming too desperate to speak much more. He holds out his hand urgently. I give him more money and he hurries off to buy dwa.

I head back to bed, not wishing to think about what I've just learned. Maybe if I just ignore it it will go away. Unfortunately my bedroom is already too hot to sleep in. I fling open the window. Outside a stallholder starts shouting about his produce and enters an argument with a customer. I shut my window in disgust. There's no getting away from the heat and the noise in Twelve Seas. I detest it.

My two Elvish clients pick this moment to visit me. As I open the door, the argument outside intensifies into a screaming match and several bystanders get involved in the uproar.

'Just ignore it,' I say, shutting the door and motioning them in. They look round at the wreckage in bewilderment.

'Just tidying up,' I say as I clear some space by kicking junk into the corners of my room. Young Kaby unfortunately chooses this moment to burst through my outside door with her boyfriend Palax in her arms. She lets him go and he falls to the ground, where he's sick on the rug.

'He's overdosed!' she wails. 'Help him.'

Out in the street people are screaming. My room is as hot as Minarixa's oven. Broken furniture is strewn everywhere. Palax's face is turning blue. Makri rushes in with a sword in her hand to see what all the fuss is about. The Elves are close to panic.

'So how are you enjoying your visit to the city?' I ask, and offer them a beer.

CHAPTER
NINETEEN

The Elves pass on the beer. Callis-ar-Del, the younger of the two, swiftly draws a pouch from his bag, crosses over to the vomiting Palax, and places a small leaf in his mouth.

'Swallow,' he orders.

Kaby brings water. Palax swallows. He stops being sick. Colour returns to his features. Callis cradles his head in his hands for a few moments, and concentrates. Palax falls asleep.

'He'll be fine now,' says the young Elf, gently releasing his head.

I'm impressed. 'You a healer?'

Callis nods, before turning to Kaby, who is squatting beside her sleeping lover, still concerned.

'Don't worry,' says the Elf. 'He will be fine. The leaf of the ledasa plant is very effective in clearing poison from the system, and I have stabilised the colours of his life energy. But he is very unwise to partake of dwa. It is an evil drug.'

'I know,' says Kaby. 'And Choirs of Angels is the worst kind. I didn't know he was taking it till I found he'd spent our week's earnings.'

Kaby and Makri carry Palax down to the caravan. I thank Callis for coming to the rescue.

'Are these ledasa leaves any good for hangovers?'

He says they are so I grab a few off him. Clever, these Elves. Talk to the trees and cure your hangover. I fill them in on the case, though in reality there isn't much to fill them in on. I tell them about my theory that the Red Elvish Cloth was inside the dragon but have to report that, if it was, it was spirited away before I got there.

They listen with interest and seem quite willing to believe my theory. Well, they have heard that I am an honest and competent man. I still like that. They take their leave, satisfied at least that I am working hard.

Makri arrives back in my room and reports that Palax seems to be out of danger.

'More than he deserves,' I say. 'He should know better than to mess with this new dwa. It's too strong. Addicts all over the city are going to be taking their usual dose and ending up dead.'

'But it feels good when you get it right,' says Makri.

I glance at her suspiciously.

'Well that's what I'm told,' she adds.

I hope she is not indulging in it herself.

'The Elves said to thank you for your help with Palax,' I tell Makri. 'They must be getting used to you.'

'Well that makes me happy as a drunken mercenary,' says Makri, wryly, and departs.

I clean up some of the mess and ask Gurd if he'll bring in a servant to do something with my rooms. He will, but it will cost me extra.

I head on out. I have an appointment at the Thamlin gymnasium, a place where aristocrats go to bathe, exercise and relax. It's a very respectable establishment. Senators and their families only. No young girls or pretty boys for hire, at least not openly. Just Senators bathing, reminiscing and talking about politics, while their sons look on respectfully. As in all gymnasia, women are not allowed, one of the many things which aggravate Makri about Turai, although she does claim that given the choice she would rather not see the naked bodies of Turai's rich and flabby upper classes.

There are some very flabby bodies here, though I'm not one to talk, and I feel self-conscious and annoyed as I'm obliged to waddle naked past young athletes disporting themselves in the water, or reclining on couches while servant rub oil into their bodies. I'd rather have kept my towel on but it's frowned upon. I feel more at home when I reach the room at the far end of the gymnasium where elderly Senators and their retinues are gathered, mostly as unfit as me. Also they have less hair. I may get mine oiled, brushed and perfumed while I'm here.

This gymnasium is, incidentally, another of Turai's architectural marvels. It has more than its fair share of splendid friezes, statues and sculptures, although I'm in no mood to appreciate them. I'm here to talk to Cerius. He doesn't want to talk to me. I drag him to a private alcove and shove him on a bench. He's long-haired and skinny and again I feel ridiculous without a good baggy tunic to cover my obesity.

'I'm working for your father.'

Cerius immediately clams up, and stares at his feet. Incongruously, he's clutching a bag of grapes, which servants distribute for free.

'Tell me about it,' I say.

Cerius remains silent and hostile. The inside of the

marble gymnasium is marginally cooler than the baking city outside, but it's still uncomfortable. I get a strong urge to walk away from this foolish young man and leap in the bathing pool. I think about my gambling debts, and try again.

'You're going to court in a week, Cerius. Dwa dealing's a serious charge. Your family's influence won't get you off, because Deputy Consul Rittius is prosecuting and he's an enemy of your father. Do you want to see your father disgraced?'

No reaction.

'You want to end up pushing an oar in a convicts' galley?'

Cerius puts a grape in his mouth. I consider slapping him. Better not, with so many Senators around. I just can't get him to speak. I don't understand it.

'Who are you protecting? The Prince? They'll find out in court, so you might as well spill it while it can do you some good.'

Cerius sits slumped in sullen silence. This is hopeless.

'I'll find out, you know. I'll study your past in the kuriya pool and see where the Choirs of Angels came from.'

All of a sudden the young man looks anguished.

'Don't!' he pleads.

'Why not? Who are you scared of?'

Cerius abruptly rises from his couch and rushes off. He leaves his bag of grapes behind. I watch him go then pick up the bag and help myself to the rest of the grapes. I notice he's been doodling on the paper. Odd, ugly shapes, scratched in ink. I rise slowly from the bench. Across the hall there's a fresco of two beautiful water nymphs frolicking with a young man with wings on his feet. He floats gracefully over the water. Lucky guy. I drag my body outside. I'm pleased to leave. All these young bodies make me feel old.

I walk down Moon and Stars Boulevard till I reach the centre of town then take a shortcut through the ruined temple of Saint Isinius. I'm passing a broken-down column when all of a sudden something smacks into the marble in front of me, sending splinters cascading around my head. I drop into a fighting crouch and spin round, sword in hand. No one's in sight. I pad softly round the column, then through the archway in front of me. Still no one. Not even a footprint in this dried-out ground. The ruins are silent and when I sniff the air I can't sense anything. Very carefully, I go back to the column. I have a shrewd idea what struck it.

Lying on the ground is a crossbow bolt, nine inches long. I stare at it, and I don't like it one bit. The crossbow is a lethal weapon, extremely powerful. It can send a bolt through solid armour, take a knight off his horse at a hundred yards. I finger the bolt uneasily, wondering who fired it. I've never heard of the Assassins using such a weapon. Nor the Society of Friends. Very strange. I place the bolt in my bag and hurry on, sword still in hand, which earns me a few funny looks when I pass out of the ruins and back into the main street beyond.

Back at the Avenging Axe, Gurd, a slow reader, is ponderously working his way through *The Renowned and Truthful Chronicle*.

'Bad weapons,' he says.

'Huh?'

'Crossbow. Brotherhood boss got killed up in Kushni

yesterday. Crossbow bolt through the neck.'

I read the report. Apparently that was the second important Brotherhood man to be killed in two days, both by crossbow. It seems like the Society of Friends might be getting the upper hand in the drug war. Aided by the mysterious crossbow wielder. It has to be the same person who shot at me. The crossbow is a specialised art. You need a serious amount of training before you can start firing bolts through people's necks from a distance.

Later Makri wonders why the Society of Friends should be firing at me. It's not like I'm on the best of terms with the Brotherhood. I can't think of an explanation. If the Society still think I've got the Red Elvish Cloth, killing me outright isn't going to get it back for them. Maybe I'm just good for some target practice.

My rooms are back in some sort of order. Time I think for a little sorcery.

CHAPTER
TWENTY

I stare at the kuriya pool with fury. I'm looking at a picture of the Fairy Glade. I presume the magic pool is once more making a fool of me. Having spent a considerable time working myself into a trance looking for information all I get is a picture of the place where my ex-wife had her assignations with the young Sorcerer. I thought it was all in the past but it must still be troubling me to interfere with the kuriya like this. Any strong image in your own mind can cause interference. Sorcerer's Apprentices often get pictures of their favourite actresses. So do Sorcerers.

This is the last of my kuriya. A waste of money. I'm about to give up in disgust when the pleasant vision of grass and flowers suddenly darkens and a malevolent face begins to take shape. I try to break the connection but it's too late, I'm trapped and I lack the power to pull away.

'Bad mistake, Thraxas,' growls the malevolent image. 'You should know better than to meddle with me.'

'And who the hell are you?' I demand.

'I am Horm the Dead.'

I cringe. My skin crawls. I'm scared. I try not to show it. 'Well, nice to meet you, Horm. But I've a few things to be getting on with—'

Horm rasps out some evil spell and my room seems to explode. I'm blinded by a searing light and flung against the wall. My desk bounces on to my chest and shards of broken glass rain down on my head as I crumple to the floor. Makri hears the noise and rushes in to find me lying hurt and confused with most of my furniture piled on top of me. She hauls the desk off me then helps me to my feet.

'What happened?'

It takes me a while to get my breath. 'A message from Horm the Dead,' I gasp, eventually.

Makri unsheathes her sword and whirls round.

'Not here. In the pool. He sent a spell through.'

'Can you do that?'

'No,' I reply. 'Well not according to what I learned anyway. I guess Horm the Dead might have some tricks we don't know in the west.'

Makri bursts out laughing.

'What's funny?'

'You're covered in ink.'

'Makri, I just suffered an attack from one of the world's most deadly Sorcerers. I don't see anything funny in that.'

This makes Makri laugh some more. 'You shouldn't have pawned your protection charm. Why is Horm trying to kill you?'

I really can't say. Just something I've blundered into as usual. But if Horm has been wrecking my room, I must have got closer to his business than he'd like.

Even Makri has heard tales of the malevolent power of Horm the Dead. 'Didn't I hear you say one time that you'd never go up against him?'

I shrug, pretending to be unconcerned. Makri is not fooled. She lectures me on the stupidity of getting involved in too many cases at once.

'You don't even know why people are trying to kill you any more.'

'I keep telling you I need the money.'

'You shouldn't have got in debt to the Brotherhood.'

'You think I don't know that? Can't you do something useful instead of lecturing me all the time?'

I hate it when I find myself involved with powerful Sorcerers. I should stick to divorce work.

Gurd is furious about the room. Destroyed three times in three days. A new record. He mutters darkly about looking for a tenant who won't keep ruining his furniture, and I have to divert him by steering the conversation round towards Tanrose, which I don't really have time for.

Later I tell Makri about the latest developments with Cerius, and the crossbow attack.

'I used the last of my kuriya looking for some clues but all I got was a vision of the Fairy Glade.'

'What's it like?'

'Like a puddle of black ink.'

'Not the kuriya, idiot. The Fairy Glade.'

'Oh. Well, it's idyllic, during the days. Fairies flying around, unicorns wandering through the trees, Nymphs and Dryads playing music, beautiful flowers, sparkling streams. You should go, Makri, you'd like it.'

'Maybe. I could use a bit of peace after living in this stinking city for a year. But Gurd says no one with Orcish blood can get in.'

This is true. The Fairy Glade is deep in the woods, a

long way from the city, and it's protected from harm by various natural magics, one of which does not allow an Orc to enter.

'You're only one quarter Orc. And you're one quarter Elf. The Fairies are big on Elves. They might take to you.'

Makri says she has had quite enough rejection from Humans to risk more at the hands of Fairies, Nymphs and Dryads.

I wonder where my wife and the young Sorcerer went after running off to the Glade all those years ago. They couldn't have stayed there long. No Human can spend a night there. Sleep comes on even if you fight it, and then the dreams drive you mad. Literally mad. Every year a few romantic or foolhardy young souls try it, and the result is always the same; they wander off to perish somewhere in the wilds or end up back in Turai begging aimlessly on street corners. The Fairy Glade is strictly for daytime visits only.

Makri says she keeps passing meetings with orators haranguing crowds in the streets, and earlier in the day she'd seen one meeting disrupted by a group of armed men.

'Election. Deputy Consul's post's coming up for grabs.'

'Why?'

'Don't you know anything about the city you live in?'

'No.'

I remember Makri hasn't been in Turai long enough to have seen an election, so I explain to her that the Deputy Consul is second only to the Consul, who's second only to the King, and that the post comes up for grabs every two years.

'The Traditionals, who support the King, always held

the post but last time Rittius won it for the Populares. Since then Lodius's party has been gaining power. Something to do with the Royal Family bleeding the city dry, no doubt. Cicerius is trying to win it back for the Traditionals.'

'So why all the fighting?' asks Makri.

'Politics is like that in Turai. No one wins an election without bribing some voters and frightening others. The Traditionals generally employ the Brotherhood as their strong-arm men and the Populares use the Society of Friends.'

Makri asks if she's entitled to vote and I tell her no, women aren't allowed, which puts her in a bad mood, even when I point out that no one is worth voting for.

'Not even the Populares? Wouldn't some democracy be a good thing?'

'It might be,' I admit. 'But we won't get it from any party with Lodius as its leader. The man's nakedly ambitious and cold as an Orc's heart into the bargain. And he's going to make a bid for power one day, whether his party wins the election or not. The King should have had him assassinated years ago.'

'Why hasn't he?'

'He left it too late and now he's scared. Lodius has powerful backing these days – rich merchants, disaffected aristocrats, ambitious generals and so on. I tell you, Makri, it's not worth getting involved.'

We play a game of niarit. I win. Makri is displeased.

'What's this?' she says, picking up a scrap of paper.

'It's a bag of grapes. Minus the grapes.'

'But it's written on.'

'Written on?' I say, studying the meaningless scribbles.

'Don't you recognise Low Orcish when you see it?'

'No. What is it?'

'The language of the Orcish underclass. Not the common Orcish tongue, or any of their national languages, but a sort of pidgin Orcish they use in the Wastelands where there are Orcs, Humans and a lot in between. They speak it in gladiator pits.'

I have to hand this one to Makri. I would've recognised standard Orcish characters but I had no idea there was a written form of pidgin Orcish.

'What's it say?'

'Load, or consignment . . . in spirit grass place. Spirit Grass Place? I don't know what that means.'

I sigh. I realise immediately what it means. 'I imagine that Spirit Grass Place is Low Orcish for the Fairy Glade, Makri. You might be getting to see it sooner than you think.'

Makri wonders out loud why Cerius, a Praetor's son, would carry around a message written in Orcish.

'I was wondering the same thing. If the Prince and Cerius are really importing dwa like Kerk says, I can't see them being involved with Orcs. Unless it's coming from Horm . . . which would explain the warning he sent me. If Cerius has got mixed up with Horm the Dead it's no wonder he's terrified. He terrifies me.'

'Is Horm a dwa dealer?'

'He could be, He uses it himself, and it's profitable enough to interest him.'

'There are two letters at the end of the message,' continues Makri. 'S and M, I think. Mean anything to you?'

I shake my head. Makri has the afternoon off from

work and is due to attend a lecture on Theological
Philosophy by Samanatius, one of Turai's leading
thinkers. Much the same as myself, I reflect, downstairs
in the bar, as I down a few beers and do some serious
thinking.

A messenger from the Brotherhood arrives. 'Yubaxas
is getting impatient,' he says.

I throw him out of the bar. 'I have two days left. Tell
Yubaxas he'll get his money.'

Spurred on to action I return to my musings about the
Cloth. I figure that I'm close somehow, and what's more,
when I find it, I'm sure I'll be able to clear the Princess.

Praetor Cicerius walks into the bar in his blue-edged
toga, to the general consternation of the assembled
drinkers. They gape in amazement as he crosses over and
greets me. Not bad, I reflect, having the Praetor himself
call on me. Might earn me a little respect round here.

Upstairs in my rooms he has some grave news. 'The
Investigator Tuparius has learned that Prince Frisen-
Akan is paying Horm the Dead to bring dwa into Turai.
Furthermore the Prince has sent a letter of credit to
cover the payment. If this becomes known to the public,
the government will fall.' The Praetor shakes his head
sadly. 'My son is involved in passing drugs from that
renegade half-Orc Sorcerer to Prince Frisen-Akan. This
is worse than anything I could have imagined. How can I
explain this to Consul Kalius? Think of the terrible
repercussions if word got out! It was bad enough before,
when the Populares merely sought to discredit me. If the
Prince is dragged into the affair, what chance do the
Traditionals have in the election?'

Cicerius insists that he does not care about winning

the post of Deputy Consul for himself, but only about the good of the city. Strangely enough, I believe him. He demands to know what I'm going to do.

'What's Tuparius going to do?' I ask.

'Nothing. After relating this information to me he was murdered on his way home. A crossbow bolt through the neck.'

'You're not making this investigation sound too attractive, Praetor. How about calling in the Civil Guard?'

'That is not possible. Many of the Guards owe allegiance to Rittius. We can't risk this scandal getting out. You will have to retrieve the letter of credit and see that the Prince's name is kept out of the affair.'

Cicerius notes my lack of enthusiasm and enquires in an acidic tone what the matter is. I point out that every man has his limits. Even me.

'If the case involves Horm the Dead, Glixius Dragon Killer and Prince Frisen-Akan, no wonder your son is scared. They scare the hell out of me. Look what happened to Tuparius. Anyway, what do you expect of me? The state should be handling the job, and is it? No, it's not, because half the forces of the state are in the pay of these people. If you want to stop Glixius Dragon Killer importing dwa from Horm the Dead, get someone else to do it.'

'I am not asking you to do any such thing.' retorts Cicerius. 'But my son must not be convicted of these charges. And Prince Frisen-Akan must not be implicated.'

'That's going to be difficult, seeing as the only way for your son to get off is by naming the Prince.'

Cicerius fixes me with his steely gaze, and demands to

know if I am aware of the importance of the affair.

'Yes. I'll probably get killed.'

'There are things more important to this city than your life, or mine,' he replies. 'If Deputy Consul Rittius succeeds in prosecuting Cerius, and disgracing the name of the Royal Family, he will win the election. If Rittius is re-elected, more Senators will move over to Lodius's party. The Populares may gain control of the Senate. Turai will be torn apart. Lodius seeks nothing less than the overthrow of the monarchy, and he will stop at nothing to procure it. He has succeeded in gathering support for his party by promising democratic reforms, but his real aim is to seize power.'

As I said, I take little interest in Turai's politics but I'm aware that Cicerius is putting forward a very one-sided view of things. Plenty of people support Senator Lodius's Populares for good reasons. The massed poor of the city have no representation in the Senate at all. The aristocrats are heavily taxed to pay for the Royal Family's luxury. Our merchants, some of whom have amassed vast wealth, are even more heavily taxed, and also have little representation, being allowed only observer status in the Senate. Among the Honourable Association of Merchants there can now be heard mutterings that, as they contribute so much in taxes to the state, they should have some say in how it's governed. This has spread to lesser guilds once renowned for fierce loyalty to the King. So the King faces an alliance of disaffected aristocrats, powerful merchants, and city artisans. He can't give in to this alliance but it's too strong for him to sweep away. Lodius has artfully harnessed these disaffections. Were I to give the matter much thought, I might well find myself in sympathy with him. After all, Turai has certainly deteriorated in the past twenty years. Unfortunately Cicerius has a trump card to play.

'Do you know that at this moment Deputy Consul Rittius is preparing a list of men who will no longer be allowed to trade in the city? Your name is on that list, Thraxas. If he is re-elected, your Investigator's licence will be withdrawn.'

I'm not sure if Cicerius is telling the truth. He might be. 'Okay, Praetor Cicerius, I'll see what I can do. You better write me an introduction.'

'An introduction?'

'To Prince Frisen-Akan. I'll have to speak to him. Don't look so appalled, Praetor. I promise I'll be polite.'

I down a few beers and head out, looking for Captain Rallee. I find him easily enough, directing the removal of a load of dead bodies from the corner of the street. Stals are fluttering around looking interested in the prospect of some profitable scavenging.

'Another attack by the Society?'

He nods. They are getting the upper hand in their war with the Brotherhood.

'It's that damned crossbow killer. He's now killed four Brotherhood bosses in the past two days.'

The Captain tells me that Choirs of Angels is flooding into the city. It's now cheaper than standard dwa.

'Won't be cheap for long, of course. Just long enough for these poor fools to get addicted.'

I mention Horm the Dead. The Captain is interested, although anything happening so far from the city is really beyond his power. No state has much control over what goes on in the Wastelands.

'The Society of Friends is cornering the market. The Brotherhood is going to have to strike back with everything they've got. Things are bad enough with the elections, without this happening as well.'

'How come the Society can get away with such a large operation?'

The Captain shrugs, which might mean anything. The higher ranks of the Civil Guard are not above corruption. Nor are senior city officials. When dealing with his superiors, Captain Rallee never knows whether or not he might be talking to someone who's raking in drug money himself. It would be practically impossible to find any person of influence in the whole city who wasn't involved in some way or other. All Captain Rallee and his guards can do is try to keep the peace, and pick up the pieces when they fail.

'Is Glixius Dragon Killer still working with the Society?' I enquire.

'We never had any proof he was working with them in the first place.'

'Well, he certainly was when he chased me through the sewers with a bunch of Society men at his back.'

The Captain shrugs again. Glixius Dragon Killer is not on any wanted list, nor can he be proved to have committed any crime. Which makes me wonder who he's bribing.

'Excuse me,' says the Captain, 'I have work to do. A gang's been robbing pilgrims out at Saint Quatinius's Shrine. Wouldn't have happened a few years back. People used to have some respect. Since half the city got hooked on dwa everything's gone to hell.'

A Civil Guard messenger thunders up on horseback and tells them they're needed fast up in Kushni where a major confrontation is again taking place between two heavily armed gangs. They depart on the double, and not long after I see Brotherhood men pouring out of the Mermaid with swords in their hands, heading north. Captain Rallee might be right. Everything *is* going to hell. What's more, the heat is absolutely unbearable.

Makri returns full of enthusiasm from the philosophy lecture given by Samanatius.

'A great man,' she enthuses.

Perspiration is running down her neck and she douses her head and shoulders with water while she tells me about the lecture. It's something to do with the nature of eternal forms, and the human soul, but most of it passes over my head.

'I asked him a question and he answered right off,' says Makri. 'Without looking at me with contempt, that is. Incidentally, I just remembered someone whose initials are S.M.'

'Pardon?'

'S.M. The Orcish initials on the bag, after the message. It might be Sarin the Merciless.'

I laugh.

'What's funny?'

'Sarin the Merciless. Sarin the Pussycat more like. I keep telling you, I ran her out of town before. She's nothing. If she's the best muscle Horm can find I've got nothing to worry about. Just start counting out my reward. Now, I'm off to see a Prince.'

CHAPTER
TWENTY-ONE

On the way home from the Palace I pass three corpses and numerous walking wounded. Two men demand to know who I'm going to vote for. I draw my sword.

'Put me down as undecided,' I growl.

On the corner of Quintessence Lane a crowd has gathered. They're looking at the young guy who sells dwa there every day. He's out of business now, with a bolt from a crossbow embedded in his neck. I have a strong appetite for four or five beers.

'How did it go?' asks Makri.

I note with disapproval that she has had her nose pierced.

'Palax and Kaby did it for me. Don't you like it?'

I shake my head. I'm too old for these outlandish fashions.

'Shouldn't you be trying to look normal, Makri, to get into the Imperial University?'

'Maybe,' she concedes. 'But I like having a ring through my nose. Do you think I should have my nipples done?'

'Who's ever going to see? You've never had a lover.'

'I might have, if all the men in Twelve Seas weren't such scum. Do you think that Elvish healer will visit again?'

'Yes. But if he finds you with your nipples pierced he'll panic. Body piercing is taboo to the Elves.'

Makri thinks she could probably change his mind. I refuse to discuss it any more.

'So what happened at the Palace? How's the Prince?'

I sigh. I can hardly bear to describe how he is. 'All the stories about Prince Frisen-Akan are true. Besides being as dumb as an Orc he's the biggest dwa addict in the city. Not to mention a stinking drunk, a thazis abuser, a hopeless gambler, a heavy debtor and all-round degenerate piece of rubbish. I look forward to his accession to the throne with great anticipation. Incidentally I'm setting out for the Fairy Glade early in the morning.'

'Why?'

'To recover the dwa the Prince is bringing into the city for Horm the Dead.'

'What?'

I shake my head and tell Makri the full sorry tale. Not only has Prince Frisen-Akan sunk so deeply into drug addiction that he barely knows what he's doing any more, he's so deeply in debt to so many people that it's becoming impossible to hush up.

'So he was planning to sell the dwa to make some money.'

Makri laughs at the thought. It is funny in a way. Some Prince.

'He was getting small amounts of the stuff from Cerius. Unfortunately that wasn't enough so he decided to try something bigger. He's putting up the money for this transaction. It's the behaviour of a lunatic – if the King finds out he'll exile him. Which wouldn't bother me a bit except the Prince dragged Cerius into this madness and if the story comes out then Cerius will probably end up taking the rap.'

'Dump your client,' advises Makri.

'I'd like to, but I can't. It's all got too complicated. If Cicerius's son goes to jail, Cicerius loses the election. If that happens, I lose my licence. Also, Cicerius has offered me much more money to intercept the dwa and bring it back safely. Or rather, bring the letter back safely.'

'What letter?'

'The letter the Prince sent authorising payment.'

Makri gapes. I gaped too when I heard about it from the Prince who, in a rare moment of lucidity, did realise that sending a letter authorising payment for six sacks of illegal drugs, and signing this letter with his own seal, wasn't the brightest thing he could have done.

If the public learns about it they might as well cancel the election. The Populares will walk it. The people of Turai will forgive the Royal Family for many things but not wholesale drug dealing with a mad Orc Sorcerer. Particularly as the Princess is at this moment awaiting trial for killing the dragon. Poor Royal Family. I'm almost starting to feel sorry for them.'

'You shouldn't get involved,' says Makri.

'Cicerius is paying me six hundred gurans if I can keep Cerius and the Prince out of it.'

'I'll go and sharpen my swords.'

We hire a couple of horses and set off early next morning. I don't know who is taking the Prince's letter of credit to the Glade, so I plan to arrive there first and intercept it. Either that or attempt to make off with the dwa myself and swap it later. Makri has her usual assortment of weapons including some small throwing stars I've never seen before.

'Assassins' weapons aren't they?'

She nods. 'I saw them on Hanama's belt that night we had the fight. I thought I'd try them out.'

The streets are still empty save for one or two dead bodies from last night's gang warfare, and the ever present beggars. I'm fairly immune to beggars now, though some of them are so pitiful it's impossible to be completely unaffected; mothers with misshapen children, men back from the wars with no legs and no army pension, hopeless itinerants going blind with cataracts in their eyes. Turai is no place to be old, sick or without friends or family. Which gives me a slightly bad feeling about my own fate. No one is going to nurse me through my dotage if I'm crippled on a case.

The Fairy Glade is a good two hours' ride from the city, east through the farmlands and the vineyards that skirt the hills. It's some way inside the huge forest that serves as the boundary between Turai and Misan, our small eastern neighbour. Nothing much goes on in Misan, which is made up of small villages and clusters of nomadic tribesmen. After that it's a few hundred miles of increasingly wild and lawless territory before you reach the lands of the Orcs.

Glixius Dragon Killer is meant to collect the Choirs of Angels from the Glade tomorrow. It's being deposited there by Horm the Dead.

'Why is the pick-up point the Fairy Glade?' asks Makri.

'Glixius insisted. He knows that as Horm is half Orc he won't be able to get into the Glade. I imagine Glixius doesn't trust him completely and wants the stuff delivered someplace he can examine it in peace without fear of Horm double-crossing him or just stealing the Prince's credit note without delivering the goods.

Somehow we've got to intercept that credit note.'

Whether or not Makri can get into the Fairy Glade remains to be seen. Whichever guardian spirits protect it, they won't be used to anyone with Orc, Elf and Human blood. I've told Makri to keep smiling and to think positive thoughts. That always pleases the Fairies.

The countryside is parched and dry. Around the city the land is irrigated with a series of small channels fed by the river but further on the fields are barren. Much of this land has been overfarmed and is becoming infertile, which is one more thing for Turai to worry about. Some way on, as the land rises gradually and the trees become more numerous, the vegetation looks rather healthier. More rain falls on these hills than falls on the city. Astrath Triple Moon explained the reason to me once but I've forgotten what it was. The vast forest is now visible on the horizon. I glance at the sky. I don't like it out here. I feel exposed in all this space. I'm too used to the city. I don't ride much these days and I'm already sore in the saddle. Makri rides without a saddle, like the Barbarian she is. She seems untroubled by the heat, even in her leather and chainmail body armour. Her axe is strapped to her saddle and her two swords form a cross on her back. We're both carrying light helmets with visors.

A small copse is in front of us, then the forest proper begins.

'I've never been in a forest before,' says Makri.

Horm the Dead rides out from the copse followed by twenty Orcish warriors.

'It might be a very short visit.'

Another twenty Orcs ride out from the trees along with a few heavily armed Humans. They encircle us. I curse myself for my carelessness but I wasn't expecting to meet Horm in person. Certainly not this side of the Glade. He must have deposited the dwa and come this way to wait for Glixius, or whoever is bringing the Prince's credit note. Makri slips her helmet over her face, takes a sword in her left hand and her axe in her right, and prepares to make her death stand. I'm still hoping to talk my way out of it.

Horm rides up. His face is deathly white and his features, not unhandsome, are immobile, set in stone. His malevolent black eyes stare at me. His thick black hair hangs round his shoulders, with dark eagle feathers woven into his plaits and black and gold beads tied into their ends. Even in this heat he's wearing his black cloak. His aura is so powerful that it's intimidating just to be near.

I put on a brave face. 'Greetings, Horm the Dead. All is well with you, I trust?'

'I warned you to stay well away from me.' He demands to know what brings me here.

'A letter of credit which the Prince very unwisely gave to Glixius Dragon Killer.'

'That is for me, not you.'

'I'm sorry, Horm. We just can't let such a thing fall into your hands. Praetor Cicerius offers to redeem it for the full amount.'

This is a lie but I'm hoping to buy some time. Horm the Dead shakes his head. He isn't interested in selling us the Prince's note.

'I have other plans for it, Thraxas. Do you think I'd be such a fool as to sell it for its face value? Once I have it in my hands the Royal Family will find themselves paying me for the rest of their lives to keep the matter quiet.'

'The King of Turai does not pay blackmailers,' I say, with dignity.

Horm the Dead laughs. 'He does if he doesn't want to be swept out of power by the Populares.'

The Orcs draw in tighter around us. They're ugly. Ugly and well armed, with scimitars and hunting bows.

'How can you dare to confront me, Thraxas? You have so little power.'

'People often say that to me. But I get by somehow.'

I've taken a small ball out of my bag.

'What is that?' sneers Horm the Dead.

'A child's toy,' I reply, and hurl it at the ground where it explodes with a flash of light and a series of powerful, reverberating crashes. The multiple firecracker causes Horm's horse to rear in terror. The Orcs behind him likewise fight to control their mounts. Makri and I need no encouragement. We're through their lines at a gallop and into the forest before anyone has time to loose an arrow at us.

'Nice move,' yells Makri, yanking her visor back to see better in the gloom.

It was a nice move. Only a smart guy like myself would know that Turanian horses are used to firecrackers because they encounter them at our festivals. To an Orc's horse from the Wastelands, it must have come as quite a surprise.

We pound along the trail, slowing as the branches droop. Behind us we hear sounds of pursuit but this forest path is a difficult place to chase anyone, as the branches are too low and the undergrowth too thick.

'How far to the Fairy Glade?'

'About a hundred yards.'

'What if I can't get in?'

'We'll plead with the fairies.'

Suddenly we burst into a clearing, a beautiful stretch of grass and flowers with a sparkling stream running down into a rocky pool. Standing beside the pool is a unicorn.

'We're here,' I say, and dismount.

'Wow,' says Makri, as the unicorn looks at us, unconcerned, and carries on drinking. I join it, scooping up some water to splash over my face.

'Is it safe?'

'Everything's safe in the Fairy Glade, Makri. Provided you don't stay the night.'

Four Fairies, each about six inches tall and wearing brightly coloured garments, flutter out of the trees and hover in front of Makri's face, examining her. Four more appear, and then more, till eventually Makri is completely surrounded by small silver-winged Fairies. They start to land on her arms, and walk over her head and shoulders.

'They like you. I thought they would.'

Somewhere a flute is playing, very gently. The Orcs can't reach us here. Strange though it seems, we forget all about them, and sit down to rest and watch the Fairies, and the unicorns and the Dryads that appear from the trees, and the Naiads that surface from the pool to play with the butterflies.

'I like this place,' says Makri, removing her body armour.

I like it too. I'm surprised. I thought I'd become too much of a cynic.

'What's that?' asks Makri as a half-man, half-horse trots into view.

'A Centaur. Pretty intelligent, by all accounts. Lascivious too.'

The Centaur approaches. Like all the magical creatures here he seems completely unconcerned by our presence. He halts in front of Makri, staring appreciatively at her curves. Makri shifts a little uncomfortably.

'Seen enough?' she says querulously, as the Centaur keeps on staring.

The Fairies giggle.

'Pardon me,' says the Centaur, pleasantly. 'Force of habit.'

He makes to leave. I remember what I'm here for. 'Excuse me,' I say. 'We're looking for some sacks of dwa.'

The Centaur frowns, and looks at me accusingly. 'Bringing such a thing into the Glade is a violation.'

'I know. That's why we're going to remove it.'

I give him a brief rundown of events, stressing heavily that myself and Makri are on the side of law and order.

'Your city's law and order mean little to us.'

'We believe in peace and love,' says Makri, which is curious coming from a woman currently carrying an axe, two swords and God knows how many knives and throwing stars. I can't imagine where Makri picked up such an odd phrase but it seems to go down well. The Centaur likes the sound of peace and love. So do the Fairies. They're clustering round Makri like bees round honey, flying round her, walking over her, playing with her hair. Obviously they love her. Makri basks in the sunshine and the attention, happy as an Elf in a tree. The Fairies don't take much notice of me.

'I'll take you to the sacks,' says the Centaur, who introduces himself as Taur. 'We will be pleased if you remove them. Although they were not prevented from entering the Glade, we did not like the people who brought them. They were Orc friends.'

We walk past the pool where the Naiads are combing their long golden tresses. The water spirits are young, beautiful and naked. Twenty years ago I'd have dived right in the pool. Oh to be young.

Taur leads us through the clearing and under the shadow of some massive old oak trees. It's so cool and pleasant that I have a strong urge to sleep. I shake it off. It's only midday but we can't waste time. We have to be out of here before nightfall.

'We're making progress,' I tell Makri. 'All we have to do is get hold of the dwa and we can trade with Glixius for the note.'

'What about Horm the Dead?'

'I don't know. I'll think of something.'

Taur takes us to the far end of the Glade and into the trees where the six sacks are partially hidden in the undergrowth. He then departs for an assignation with a Dryad. I'm almost moved to smile. Mission accomplished, as my old Commanding Officer used to say. Now I'm in a position to trade for the letter of credit. The Fairies stay with Makri while we load the sacks of dwa on to our horses.

'How do we get out of here?' enquires Makri. 'I don't mind fighting forty Orcs but I can't guarantee I'll kill every one of them.'

'You disappoint me. As they can't get in here, maybe we could stay just inside the boundary and pick them off? If we killed enough of them we could make a run for it.'

Makri pulls out her throwing stars. 'We might get a few of them. But Orcs aren't that stupid. Once they see what's happening they'll just withdraw far enough away that we can't reach them.'

'Do you have a better idea?'

'No.'

'So we might as well try it.'

We hurry back to the clearing where our horses engage briefly in conversation with two Centaurs who greet us affably as we pass. It's strange being surrounded by these peculiar creatures, all of them without a care in the world, while our lives are in such extreme danger. We creep through the trees to the edge of the Glade, then separate. I get down on my belly and crawl forward, trying to spot the line of sentries. There's no sign of any. I can't find an Orc anywhere. Makri returns with the same tale. The Orcs are not guarding the Glade.

'Strange. They must be waiting outside the forest, watching the paths.'

'I know this forest,' I say, gaining confidence. 'I can lead us north and out of the forest far away from the path. We'll be back in Turai before they know we've gone.'

I'm surprised at such poor tactics from an experienced warrior like Horm the Dead. Dwa must be addling his mind. We hurry to make our escape. The Fairies still flutter along happily beside Makri. They seem to be enjoying it all. Centaurs call out appreciatively as we reach the clearing. Taur, back from his assignation, is just making some gracious comments about Makri's figure when he stops short, tossing his head in alarm and sniffing the air. The hairs on the back of my neck start to prickle. I can sense something very bad about to happen.

'What is it?' asks Makri.

'Horm the Dead. He's close.'

'Horm can't get in here!'

I look up, shielding my eyes against the burning sun.

High above, a monstrous shape is circling the Glade. As it descends its great wings beat the air like a vision of hell. The Centaurs wail. The Fairies shriek and fly into the trees and the Naiads disappear under the water. Horm the Dead and thirty Orcs are gliding towards us on the back of a dragon. A real war dragon. Not a small one like the one in the King's zoo. Not a half-grown thing like the one Makri fought in the slave pits. A proper Orcish war dragon, black and gold, vast in size, with terrible fangs, fiery breath, scales like armour and talons that can tear a man in two. The most frightening creature ever to draw breath, and it's coming our way, fast.

'A war dragon,' I say to Makri. 'God knows how Horm got hold of it but it looks like he's decided to smash his way into the Glade.'

Makri stands firm with her axe raised. 'I fought one before . . .'

The dragon circles closer.

'It was an awful lot smaller than that though,' she admits. 'Did you and Gurd really kill a dragon in the war?'

'Yes. Not nearly as big as this though, and the sleep spell gave us a couple of seconds to get its eyes. But you can't use magic here. My sleep spell won't work in the Fairy Glade.'

'It's funny the way your spells tend not to work whenever we need them most.'

'Yes, I've noticed that as well.'

As the dragon nears we see that it's wearing a visor of steel mesh to protect its eyes. When the dragon is about fifty feet above the ground, and Horm and his troops are screaming at us and brandishing their swords, there's a terrific flash of lighting as it hits the protective magical field that covers the Glade. The dragon screams and a blast of flame belches from its nostrils. One Orc plummets to the ground but the rest hang on grimly, as the dragon furiously throws itself against the barrier. It screams and writhes, beating at the air with its wings and talons. Bolts of blue lightning split the sky and thunderous explosions rock the Glade. A tremendous flash lights up the forest as the barrier finally gives way. The vast golden bulk of the beast crashes to the ground and lies stunned in a great cloud of smoke and dust. There's a brief moment of silence, then with fierce war cries the Orcs emerge like demons from the smoke, and charge towards us, waving their swords and screaming.

I turn to flee. Makri stands her ground. I curse at her, and grab her arm. She brushes me off.

'I'm not running from Orcs twice in one day,' she declares, gripping her axe and slipping on her helmet. Neither of us has had time to don our armour so Makri faces the charge wearing only her chainmail bikini and helmet whilst I'm standing in an undershirt hoping no one shoots an arrow into my belly.

An amazing thing happens. A great phalanx of fabulous creatures emerges from the trees, ready to fight to defend the Fairy Glade from the hated Orcs. Centaurs, unicorns and Dryads, with clubs and spears, rush forward to meet the Orcs' charge. The air is thick with furious, spitting Fairies, and odd Pixie-like creatures that ride on the backs of the Centaurs, brandishing knives.

Battle is joined. The Glade dwellers plus myself and Makri against thirty huge Orc warriors and the malevolently powerful Horm the Dead. Thank God the dragon is stunned. The air still crackles as Horm attempts to force his sorcery to work in the magic-dampening space around him. Bolts of lightning flicker from his fingers, powerful enough to drive back the Centaurs but not yet strong enough to spread destruction. The Orcs attempt to slash their way through us and their huge curved blades inflict some damage but they're driven back by stabbing unicorns and clubbing Centaurs, and Fairies who fly round them spitting in their eyes and pricking them with tiny, needle-like weapons.

Makri starts hacking her way through towards the Orc Commander, a huge creature with two massive swords who rallies his forces with an evil, screeching battle cry. I'm confronted by two Orcs and forced sideways against a tree. I manage to strike one of them down and before the other can attack he's transfixed from behind by a unicorn's horn.

Horm the Dead is not one of those Sorcerers who shuns battle. Seeing his Orcs hard pressed, he abandons his effort to work his magic and lays about him with a black sword to murderous effect. He sends a Naiad flying backwards screaming and almost decapitates a Centaur with a great curving blow. In the midst of the mayhem, I glimpse some naked Naiads emerging from the water and swiftly dragging the bleeding Dryad away from the scene and into the pool.

The forces of the Fairy Glade have the Orcs out-numbered. We start to outflank them, forcing the Orcs to retreat towards the still unconscious dragon. The Orcs form up in front of the gigantic, smoking beast, using its bulk to guard their backs. Fighting is extremely fierce. The Glade beings lose some momentum in the face of determined Orcish resistance, and the outcome hangs in the balance. Then Makri slays an Orcish warrior and bursts through their ranks to mount a furious attack on their Commander. He roars an Orcish curse at her and assails her with his two huge swords. Makri parries with her axe and sword, screams a curse of her own, and buries her axe deep in his helmet. The Centaurs cheer and charge forward with their clubs and the Fairies renew their efforts at confusing their enemies, buzzing and stabbing like a horde of tormenting insects.

The Orcs crumble under our final assault and are hacked down in front of the dragon. Horm the Dead, streaming with blood, screams in rage as he holds off Makri and a Centaur. Summoning one last great burst of energy, he shouts out a demonic spell and the air around him crackles with fire as the spell struggles against the magic dampening aura of the Fairy Glade. Finally it bursts through, sending Makri and the others spinning backwards. Horm screams a desperate command to the dragon, causing it to rouse itself with a terrifying roar. Makri picks herself up and sprints back towards the Sorcerer, but before she can reach him he scales the side of the dragon and orders it into the air. With a great beating of its wings the huge war dragon lifts off the ground. Makri, frustrated by the escape, whips a throwing star from her bag and hurls it at Horm. He screams as it embeds itself in his leg, but he hangs on. There's another terrific flash of blue lightning as the dragon crashes up out of the magical field leaving thirty dead Orcs below, and not a few casualties on our side.

We've won. Thraxas, Makri and the unicorns beat off Horm and a dragon. When I tell them about it at the Avenging Axe, they'll never believe me.

I'm completely drained. I can barely stand. I haven't been in a battle like that for a long time. I slump to the ground. The Centaurs and their friends take no rest, but immediately start dragging their wounded companions towards the pool. When I see the first badly wounded Dryad emerge healthily from the water just moments later I understand that the water has healing powers, and will protect the inhabitants of the Glade.

Makri has some wounds of her own. She has a gash on her arm and her nose is torn and bleeding where an Orcish blade ripped out her nose ring.

'Damn,' she says, and winces in pain.

Taur trots over. He's looking pleased with himself.

'A fine battle,' he says, as he scoops up water from the pool to rub on Makri's wounds. He carries on rubbing longer than is strictly necessary, but the bleeding stops, and Makri starts to heal right before our eyes.

'You have a strong constitution,' says Taur. 'And a fine body. Are you planning on staying?'

'Won't it drive me mad?'

'It drives Humans mad. But I'm sure that a woman of your extraordinary make-up would be quite safe.'

'You hear that, Thraxas? A woman of my extraordinary make-up.'

I snort. I'm getting fed up with this. She declines Taur's offer however, telling him that she must get back to the city. The Centaur is disappointed.

'Visit us again soon,' he says.

'We love you,' say the Fairies, and settle on her shoulders. Makri is happy as an Elf in a tree. A pleasant visit to the Fairy Glade and a good battle all in one day. She's particularly pleased to have killed the Orcish Commander.

'I knew him when I was a slave,' she tells us. 'He badly needed killing.'

I drink plenty of water from the pool. Makri declares it to be the most refreshing thing she's ever tasted. I'm not entirely satisfied.

'Got any beer?' I ask Taur as we saddle up our horses.

His eyes twinkle. 'Not exactly, Thraxas, but we do have some fine mead.'

Mead. Alcohol made from honey. Not one of my favourites, but better than nothing I suppose. I accept the flagon from Taur and the rest of the Glade dwellers look kindly on us as we depart. They like us for helping protect the Glade against the Orcs, and for removing the dwa from their presence.

'Visit us again,' calls Taur to Makri, waving goodbye.

She waves farewell.

'You know, given that you're a social outcast in polite society, it's amazing the way some people take to you, Makri,' I say, as we ride out into the forest path.

'Well, the Centaurs certainly liked me,' agrees Makri. 'And the Fairies. But they liked you too, I saw some of them resting on you.'

'They were using my belly as a sunshade.'

I guzzle down some mead. It tastes sweet; not unpleasant though no substitute for beer, and not nearly potent enough after my recent experiences.

'You want to be careful,' says Makri. 'We have a long way to ride and I don't want you falling off your horse.'

'Pah,' I snort, and drink more from the flagon. 'It'll take more than Fairy juice to affect me.'

By the time we're halfway home I am spectacularly, roaringly, hopelessly drunk. Taur's mead is obviously more powerful than I thought. As we pass some farm labourers I brandish my sword and sing a battle song to them. They laugh, and wave back genially. We pass through some lightly wooded hills and I let go with another fine old drinking song. Suddenly I feel overwhelmingly tired and fall off my horse. There is a loud thwack as something thuds into a tree next to me.

'What—?'

Makri leans over. 'A crossbow bolt!'

It occurs to me, none too clearly, that it would have hit me had I not at that precise moment had the good fortune to fall off my horse.

I struggle to my feet. The bolt is embedded deep in the tree. Makri leaps from her horse, swords at the ready, and crouches watchfully. I grab my own sword and try to pull myself together.

A figure steps out from the trees to our right, a crossbow in his hands. He walks towards us with the shaft pointing at Makri. Fifteen feet away from us he halts. It's not a him, it's a her. A tall woman, plainly dressed, with her hair cropped very short, wearing, for some reason, a great many earrings. She turns her gaze on me.

'You drunken oaf, Thraxas,' she says, with some contempt.

'A friend of yours?' enquires Makri, who is crouched ready to spring.

'I never saw her before.'

'You have. I looked rather different then. I am Sarin. Sarin the Merciless. And you would be one dead Investigator if you hadn't fallen off your horse.'

She laughs, mirthlessly. 'But I can soon fix that.'

Sensing Makri about to spring, she instantly turns the crossbow on her.

I can't quite make this out. Sarin the Merciless never used to be a deadly woman with a crossbow. Must have been taking lessons. I curse myself for drinking so much mead, and shake my head to clear it.

'What do you want?'

She fixes me with a stare. Her eyes are black and cold as an Orc's heart. This is not the same woman I remember at all.

'You dead would be a good start, drunkard. But that can wait. Right now I'll take the dwa.'

Her black eyes flicker back to Makri.

'The Fairies liked you,' says Sarin. 'Strange. They didn't seem to take to me.

'They didn't like me either,' I growl. 'They probably guessed I've got a terrible temper. So get out of my way.'

Sarin pulls something from her tunic. 'I take it you are hoping to trade the dwa for this?'

It's the Prince's credit note, but Sarin doesn't seem keen to enter into negotiations.

'I've decided I might as well keep the note and take the dwa. Now hand it over. I'm very good with this crossbow.

I'd say you're at my mercy. As you may know, that is not something I have much of.'

She laughs.

Unfortunately Makri is not the sort of person you can rob and expect to put up no resistance. Her fighting code, not to mention her pride, just won't allow it. Any second now I can tell that she is either going to leap at Sarin or try and catch her with a throwing star or knife before she can shoot. I don't like this too well. Sarin the Merciless has proved she's skilful with that crossbow, and I'm not sure that she might not transfix Makri before she could come to grips.

A terrible wave of tiredness passes over me. Delayed shock from the war dragon. Or just too much mead. I take a quick decision to act before things get out of hand. I'm still carrying the sleep spell. I'll take Sarin out before she can do any harm. The fatigue is overwhelming. I can hardly stand. I bark out the spell. Makri looks briefly surprised, then crumples gently to the ground. I realise that I have rather messed things up. The effort of casting the spell finishes me off. I fall to the ground. The last thing I hear before passing out is Sarin's mocking laughter.

An Elf is standing over me. It's Callis, brandishing a lesada leaf. He must have guessed I've been drinking. I wash it down and struggle to my feet. Makri is still sleeping gently on the grass. Jaris has rounded up our horses and is leading them over.

'What happened?' asks Callis, as he goes to attend to Makri. I decline to comment. Callis tells me that when he appeared a tall woman was in the process of loading sacks on to her horse.

'She rode off. Was it the Cloth?' he asks.

'No. Something else. But related to your case,' I add, just in case he thinks I'm not working hard enough for him. I curse. Everything has gone wrong. Now Sarin the Merciless has the dwa and the letter. It's just as well the Elves appeared before she used my sleeping figure for target practice. I wonder why the Elves did happen along, and ask them.

'We were looking for you,' explains Callis. 'Gurd at the Avenging Axe told us that you had gone to confront Horm the Dead and we wished to help. Even in the Elvish Lands Horm has an evil reputation.

Makri wakes suddenly and leaps to her feet with a savage snarl and a sword in each hand. She looks round in confusion, wondering where the enemy is. When the realisation of what happened sinks in she is angrier than I've ever seen her. The Elves watch in bemusement as she berates me at length at my utter stupidity in misdirecting my sleep spell, sending her instead of Sarin crashing to the ground.

I can think of little to say in my defence and am forced to listen to her rage about my drunkenness, incompetence and general stupidity, after which she proceeds to fume about the disgrace to her fighting honour.

'I met sub-Human Trolls in the gladiator pits who were smarter than you! Number one chariot, are you? Sarin would have stuck you full of holes if the Elves hadn't rescued you. You're about as much use as a one-legged gladiator. You made me fall asleep in front of an opponent!' she yells. 'I'll never live it down. That's it, I'm finished. Next time you want some help, don't bother asking, I'm busy.'

And with that she leaps on her horse and gallops off without even acknowledging the Elves' presence. They look at me wonderingly.

'A very volatile character,' I say, waving my hands in vague explanation. 'Takes defeat too personally.'

I ride back to Turai with the Elves. They are puzzled that a fine sorcerous Investigator like myself could actually misdirect a spell, thereby putting his companion to sleep, but after I explain about Sarin's own considerable sorcerous powers, and the spells she was throwing at me right and left, I don't think their confidence in me is shaken too badly.

Next morning I wake with the mother of all hangovers, the Brotherhood beating on my door, and the city in violent uproar. Once again it is a poor start to the day.

'Money's due tomorrow,' says Karlox.

'Fine,' I grunt, avoiding some flying debris. 'It'll be there. Which is more than you'll be if the Society of Friends keeps picking you off.'

Karlox snarls. He doesn't like that. 'We got their measure. And we got yours. You don't pay up tomorrow, you better make sure you've been saying your prayers.'

I slam the door on him.

I don't say my prayers but it doesn't prevent young Pontifex Derlex from visiting me right after the riot calms down. The sun is beating down more ferociously than ever, making him sweat inside his black religious robe, but he declines my offer of a beer. The Pontifex is doing the rounds in his constituency, checking up on people after the riot. Makri pushes her head through the outside doorway and is about to say something when she notices the Pontifex and clams up. She departs. I notice Derlex's deep frown.

'Loosen up, Derlex. No need to look like your soul's in torment every time you catch sight of Makri.'

He apologises, rather stiffly, but admits that Makri does make him very uncomfortable. 'The Orcish blood, you know.'

'She's got Human blood as well. Elf too. Probably a very interesting soul. You should try and convert her.'

He looks uncomfortable again. 'I don't think I am allowed to try. It's blasphemous to preach the True Religion to an Orc . . . even one quarter Orc might involve me in some heresy . . .'

I laugh at the thought, and tell him not to worry. Makri is not in line for any sudden conversion. After a little talk about this and that, he goes on his way.

I wander out into the corridor. A thought strikes me suddenly. Makri appears, heading downstairs for her first shift of the day. I ask her what she wanted earlier.

'To tell you never to speak to me again. Or communicate in any way. From now on, Thraxas, you don't exist.'

'Makri—'

She walks stiffly past, tossing her head so that her long hair swings around her shoulders. Obviously she has not yet forgiven me for yesterday's escapade.

'It could have happened to anyone!' I yell at her departing form. Now I'm distracted. What was I thinking about? The True Church. Something about it is nagging me.

Downstairs I sit over a beer and a plate of stew and think things over. Why did Derlex visit me? Plenty of other people in riot-torn Twelve Seas must need his help more than me. Now I think about it, Derlex never stops visiting me these days. I never used to see him from one year to the next. What made the Church so interested in my welfare all of a sudden?

Thinking about the Church nudges my memory along and I realise what it is that's been bugging me. Pazaz. The Orc dragonkeeper. He said that no one spoke to him, apart from Bishop Gzekius. According to Pazaz, Gzekius tried to convert him.

'But that's impossible,' I say, out loud to no one. 'Derlex just told me it was blasphemous to preach the True Religion to an Orc. The Bishop couldn't have been trying to convert him. He's not going to lay himself open to a heresy charge just for one dragonkeeper. The other Bishops would be down on him like a bad spell.'

I stand up, banging my fist on the table. Makri looks at me very coolly.

'That's it! That's why Derlex has been round here all the time. He's spying on me for the Bishop. And the Bishop is after the Cloth! The Church is behind it all! The Royal Family was attending some special religious service when the dragon was cut open. Which means that the Church would know exactly when the zoo was going to be empty. And the Bishop was talking to the dragonkeeper before that. He wasn't trying to convert him. He was pumping him for information! Just like Derlex has been round here pumping me for information! Derlex was at the Palace that day; he rode home with us in the landus. He probably had the Cloth on him then, passed to him by some other Churchman. And now I think about it, when I returned to Attilan's house to retrieve the spell there was another young Pontifex passing by. He could have stolen the spell, just before I came looking for it.'

Makri raises her eyebrows. Sweat is running down her body, making her muscles glisten. She's been listening, but still refuses to acknowledge me.

I wonder why the Church would want the Elvish Cloth. There could be any number of reasons. Maybe just to sell it. Or perhaps the Bishop needs to do some secret planning without getting spied on by the other Bishops. Gzekius is an ambitious man, it's about time he made a try for the Archbishopric. It seems to fit together well enough. And if I'm right, then the Red Elvish Cloth should be somewhere in the Church's possession right now.

'It might even be in Derlex's church. And if it is, I'm going to find it! Are you free tonight?'

Makri glowers at me. 'No. I'm studying. You're on your own.'

She grabs a tablecloth, savagely wipes a few tables, then stalks off through the back to bring in a box of tankards. Tanrose appears carrying a large chunk of beef for the lunchtime stew. I buy a pastry and tell her about Makri being mad at me. Tanrose already knows all about it.

'She's angrier than a Troll with a toothache,' says Tanrose. 'But she'll get over it.'

'I need her help tonight. Any suggestions for helping her get over it quickly?'

'Bring her some flowers,' says the cook.

The suggestion is so strange that at first I fail to grasp what she means. 'Flowers? What for?'

'To say sorry of course.'

'Say sorry with flowers? To Makri? You mean go out and buy some flowers and give them to Makri as a present? As a way of saying sorry? Flowers?'

'That's right.'

'Are we talking about the same Makri here? Makri the axe woman?'

'Just because a woman wields an axe doesn't mean she wouldn't appreciate a bunch of flowers.'

'She'd probably attack me with them.'

'You'd be surprised,' says Tanrose, and gets on with hacking up the lump of beef.

Tanrose must be losing her mind. Flowers for Makri, indeed! The idea makes my head hurt. Right then Praetor Cicerius walks in, accompanied by the Consul himself. Well, well. I certainly get a higher class of visitor these days.

Cicerius tersely relates that the city is fast degenerating into chaos. The fighting between the Brotherhood and the Society of Friends has reached new heights and the Civil Guard is losing control.

'I've advised the King to suspend the constitution,' says Consul Kalius, 'and send in the Army.'

I imagine the King will be hesitant to do this. The Populares might come out in open revolution. Various generals are suspected of being supporters of Senator Lodius, and there's no knowing how obedient the Army would be.

'We're facing complete anarchy,' complains Cicerius. 'The Traditionals must retain power if the city is to survive. Did you get the letter?'

I admit that I didn't. This doesn't go down too well. I relate the events of the previous day, more or less. I don't explain exactly how Sarin the Merciless ended up with the dwa and the letter. Cicerius and Kalius are aghast and berate me for my failure. The Consul openly implies that I'm fabricating the whole story about the dragon in the Fairy Glade just to make my failure look better, and wonders out loud if I might not have sold the dwa for myself.

I haven't had enough sleep. I never get enough sleep. It's hot as Orcish hell in here. My head is pounding. I can't take much more of this. I point to the door and order them to leave. The Consul is shocked. As Turai's most powerful administrator, he's not used to being shown the door.

'How dare you!' he rages.

'Why not? I'm a free man. I don't have to listen to anyone calling me a liar, even the Consul. Especially when I've got a headache. I did my best. If that best isn't good enough, then tough. Now leave.'

Cicerius waves this away. 'This is no time for squabbling,' he states. 'If the Society of Friends obtains—'

I wave him quiet. I'm in no mood for speeches. 'I know. Prince disgraced, your son disgraced. Traditionals disgraced, you lose election, Populares win, Lodius marches to power. That's the scenario according to you. I've heard it before. What do you expect me to do?'

'Find the letter,' says the Praetor.

'I already failed.'

'Then you must try again. Don't forget, my son Cerius is your client. The letter will send him to prison.'

I frown. I hate the way Cicerius keeps pulling the 'can't desert a client' routine. I wish I'd never heard of the damn client. It's too hot to think clearly. What will Sarin the Merciless do with the damning letter of credit? She won't have any interest in using it for political means but she'll certainly know how valuable it is to the King's opponents. The Populares are the obvious people to sell it to, and easy for her to reach, because Senator Lodius is supported by the Society of Friends, and Sarin's associate Glixius is himself associated with the Society. I don't even know if they are still working together. It seems like Sarin might have gone off on her own. Double-crossing your associates is standard behaviour in the Turanian underworld.

'We still might be able to buy it back, but it would cost you plenty to outbid the Society. Be better if we could just steal it. Haven't your Sorcerers been able to locate her? She's carrying six bags of dwa. Someone should be able to pick up the aura.'

'Tas of the Eastern Lightning has scanned the city without finding anything.'

Tas of the Eastern Lightning has taken over from the murdered Mirius Eagle Rider as the Chief Sorcerer at Palace Security. He's powerful enough. If he can't find it by magic, probably no one can.

The call for morning prayers resonates through the city. The Consul and the Praetor are less than pleased to be obliged to kneel and pray in a tavern, but there's no getting out of it. I find myself kneeling in prayer beside a blue-edged toga and a gold-edged one. I notice my own tunic is frayed. I wonder if my prayers will have some extra effect, seeing as they're being offered up in such high-powered company. Afterwards we discuss things for a while and I agree to do my utmost to locate Sarin. They depart, still brushing the dust from their knees.

Makri reappears and starts cleaning the debris off the floor. I appeal to her better nature and tell her I could really do with some help tonight. She refuses to talk, and practically sweeps me up with the rubbish. I catch Tanrose looking at me from behind a vast cauldron of beef stew.

'To hell with this,' I grunt, and storm out the front entrance. Baxos the flower seller has plied his trade on the corner of Quintessence Street for thirty years. I estimate it is twenty years at least since I availed myself of his services. He practically falls over in surprise when I march up and demand a bunch of flowers.

'Hey Rox,' he calls over to a fish vendor on the other side of the road. 'Thraxas is buying some flowers.'

'Got a lady friend, has he?' yells back Rox, loud enough for the entire street to hear.

'Time you were courting again, Thraxas!' screams Birix, one of Twelve Seas' busier prostitutes. The cry is taken up enthusiastically by her companions.

I grab a bunch of flowers, toss some pennies at Rox and march off hastily, pursued by a great deal of ribald witticisms. I am in the foulest of tempers and will have more than a few harsh words to say to that idiot Tanrose.

Back at the Avenging Axe I practically crash into Makri and her mop. I thrust the flowers into her hand, figuring it's best to get it over with quickly.

'I'm sorry I put you to sleep in front of an opponent,' I say. 'Here are some flowers.'

Makri gawps in amazement while I march swiftly onwards to the bar for a much needed flagon of ale.

Almost immediately I am tapped on the shoulder. It's Makri, who then proceeds to do a number of strange things. First she embraces me, then she burst into tears, and runs out of the room.

I'm bewildered. 'What's happening?'

'The apology worked,' replies Tanrose, in a satisfied manner.

'Are you sure?'

'Of course I'm sure.'

'It all seems very strange to me, Tanrose.'

'I wasn't surprised your marriage broke up, Thraxas,' says Tanrose, as she shovels some stew on to a plate for me.

CHAPTER
TWENTY-FOUR

I spend the afternoon drinking a few beers, thinking things over, and swapping tales with a mercenary from the far north. He passed through Nioj on his way to Turai and from his account it sounds as if the Niojans are preparing for war.

'They say they heard some rumours that some Orcs were marauding on the borders.'

It could be true. Or it could be a story put about to deceive our King into thinking they weren't about to attack us. It's bound to happen some time, and they still have the excuse of their murdered diplomat. Cities have fallen on flimsier excuses than that.

Could the Church have murdered him? Would Bishop Gzekius go that far? Maybe. I have no other candidates in mind.

Makri returns from her lunchtime logic class. She does appear to have been pacified by the flowers. Apparently no one ever gave her flowers before. Smart idea from Tanrose, I must admit, though Makri is embarrassed at bursting into tears and instructs myself and Tanrose never to mention it to anyone.

Makri reports that things are pretty grim outside. She had to fight her way through three street brawls on the way to the Guild College.

'I have a lecture in mathematics this afternoon,' she says. 'I'd better sharpen my axe before I go. Incidentally, Sarin the Merciless didn't seem quite so useless as you made her out to be.'

'She got lucky. She's learned how to use a crossbow. Big deal. Just wait till I meet her again. I suppose I will, now the Consul wants me to find her. But it's going to have to wait because I'm going looking for the Red Elvish Cloth. Which is just as well maybe, because I've no idea where Sarin is. If Tas of the Eastern Lightning can't find her, how do they expect me to? I wonder if Rittius is really planning to take away my licence. Cicerius might just be saying that to scare me. You know it's rumoured Rittius is going to introduce a bill banning the Association of Gentlewomen?'

Makri nods. She attended an A.G. meeting last night and as a consequence has now gathered further knowledge of Turanian politics.

'It's confusing,' she admits. 'Some powerful women in the city are already campaigning behind the scenes against Rittius because he's against the Association. But a lot of the Association of Gentlewomen still support the Populares because they'd like to see some reform. The meeting ended with everyone arguing.'

'I'm not surprised. No one in Turai can ever agree about politics. I'd like to take a holiday till it's all over.'

'Where?'

'Anywhere I'm not wanted by the law. Which does limit the choice, now I think about it. I've violated statutes in every neighbouring state. Maybe I could travel to the furthest west and see what Kamara is like.'

'It's not like you to admit defeat, Thraxas.'

'I know. But I really can't think how to find Sarin. If Tas can't find her, then no magic of mine or even Astrath's is going to be any good. And I've got no influence in the north of the City. If she's with the Society, I'll never reach her.'

A messenger arrives for me, bearing a brief note: '*Come alone to the Stadium Superbius at midnight if you want to bid for the letter,*' it says. It's signed by Sarin the Merciless.

'I suppose that simplifies things,' I admit. 'Might end up a good day after all. Burgle Derlex's church tonight and pick up the Cloth, then move on and buy the letter from Sarin. With any luck I'll be paying off the Brotherhood tomorrow.'

CHAPTER TWENTY-FIVE

'Feel like going to church, Makri?'

'If we must.'

The streets are quiet, barely illuminated by the oil lamps on each corner. The whores have all gone home, and the only people in sight are the homeless beggars who sleep in doorways.

We make our way down to the end of Saint Volinius's Street, right by the docks. Behind us the huge hulks of triremes and quinquiremes float high in the water, ready to take on cargo tomorrow. The sight makes me pause. I saw a fair amount of the known world in my younger days, but it's been a good many years since I've travelled far from Turai. What would it be like, I wonder, to get on a ship and sail to Samsarina or Simnia in the west? Or further, to the distant, barely explored shores of Kastlin? South perhaps, to the Elvish Islands, where the sun shines on perfect white beaches and music floats through the trees? I shake my head. I'm too old to go travelling again. I guess I'll be stuck in this city for the rest of my life.

In front of us is the large and imposing Church of Saint Volinius, the only richly decorated building in Twelve Seas. So far the dwa addicts haven't started robbing the churches. It's only a matter of time. No lights show though a lamp is visible in the window of the small house in the grounds where the Pontifex lives. We hurry to the back of the church. I hesitate. I've never broken into a church before and I don't relish the prospect. Just because I can't be bothered praying doesn't mean I relish offending the Divinity.

Makri sees my hesitation.

'If someone finds us here and I cut their head off the Divinity will be far more offended,' she says, encouragingly.

I mutter the opening incantation. Nothing happens. Not surprising. You'd expect a Pontifex like Derlex to know the common minor incantations, even if the Church does disapprove of magic.

'Locking spell,' I mutter, and get to work. It doesn't take long. I was picking locks as soon as I could walk. I have a natural talent for it. We hurry inside. Makri takes one of the huge candles off the altar and lights it from her tinderbox. I get the impression she's enjoying this sacrilegious behaviour but it's making me uneasy. Shadows from the statues around us loom out eerily as we pass and I half expect some ancient saint to step out from an alcove and reprimand me for desecrating church property.

We start to hunt, lifting up the altar cloth, peering under the pews, poking around in all the nooks and crannies of the church. We haven't got very far when we are interrupted by a faint noise from the door we came in. Makri swiftly blows out the candle and we disappear silently under a pew. A tiny glimmer of light flickers into view. I risk a quick glance, then put my mouth to Makri's ear.

'Glixius,' I whisper. 'And three others.'

Concealed under the bench, we wait as the Sorcerer and the Society of Friends search the church. Obviously

I am not the only person who suspects the True Church of the theft.

Again noises come from the door. Glixius's illuminated staff is extinguished and the four men conceal themselves somewhere in the far side of the church. I peek out from my hiding place. Entering the building, sword in hand, is Hanama. Watching her creep silently towards the altar I am again mystified by the Assassins' interest in the Cloth.

Hanama has even less time to search than Glixius. She is interrupted almost immediately by the sound of yet another party entering, and swiftly conceals herself behind the altar, disappearing only seconds before Yubaxas and five Brotherhood men steal silently into the church.

'I think I'm going to laugh,' whispers Makri.

I shoot her a warning glance, though I have to admit it is funny in a grim sort of way. With us, the Society of Friends and an Assassin all hiding under chairs and suchlike, it's starting to remind me of one of the sillier comedies at the theatre.

When sounds of entry force Yubaxas and his companions to scurry for cover, Makri actually does giggle, though this is fortunately covered up by the voices of the new arrivals who are making no effort to be silent. A quick glance reveals Bishop Gzekius and four Curates with lanterns, led in by Pontifex Derlex.

'Where is it?' demands Gzekius, his voice booming through the church.

Derlex unlocks a side room. They enter, and emerge quickly with a large piece of folded Red Cloth.

'Excellent,' says the Bishop.

I wait tensely. Are any of the people hiding here about to rob the Bishop? I certainly do not intend to, not even to clear the Princess's name and claim the huge reward. I'd be in endless trouble afterwards. It's disappointing that so many others worked out where the Red Elvish Cloth was, but I can live with the disappointment. It's better than being hauled up in court for burglary, and probably heresy and treason as well.

The back door flies open. Shockingly, four Orcs stride in. The Bishop cries out in horror. Orcs are quite definitely not allowed in a true church. I groan. I know what's going to happen now, but I'm powerless to prevent it. Makri leaps from under the pew and hurtles towards the Orcs, a sword in each hand and murder in her eyes. I drag myself to my feet and run after her. I can't let her fight four Orcs on her own.

'Thraxas!' yells Pontifex Derlex.

'Orcs!' screams Yubaxas, as the Brotherhood reveal themselves.

It goes badly for the Orcs. Makri and I engage with them while the Brotherhood and Hanama outflank them. Even the Curates lend a hand. The Orcs are quickly cut down.

'Orcish scum,' spits Makri, and kicks one of the bodies.

'What are you doing here?' screams Bishop Gzekius.

Personally I'm stuck for an answer. The awkward silence doesn't last long. There's a huge thunder flash and everyone except me is flung to the floor. I remain upright, if shaky. One advantage of carrying a lot of weight – good centre of balance. Glixius Dragon Killer has emerged to enter the fray. He makes straight for the Cloth.

'I notice you didn't come out to fight the Orcs,' I say as

he advances, and grab the Red Elvish Cloth from the floor.

'Allies come and allies go. Now give me that!' he shouts.

'Blasphemers!' yells Bishop Gzekius. 'You'll all pay for this! Get out of my church!'

Glixius lunges at me. Makri sticks out her leg and he crashes to the floor. I take the Bishop's advice, and flee with the Cloth.

By the time I reach the alley outside Makri is at my shoulder and we're about fifteen seconds in front of Glixius and the Society of Friends.

'Look!' gasps Makri. At the far end of the dark alley are eight armed men.

Makri's swords appear in her hands.

'We're trapped,' I groan.

Bizarrely, a manhole cover opens in front of us.

'In here!' hisses a voice.

It's Hanama. Typically, she slipped out of the Church unnoticed.

I hesitate. Meeting Assassins in sewers isn't all that attractive a prospect. And I haven't forgotten the alligator. Suddenly my senses go crazy. Glixius Dragon Killer has rounded the corner and is about to unleash a ferocious spell. I unfurl the roll of Cloth in an instant and hurl it over myself and Makri. The spell bounces harmlessly off us but Makri, taken by surprise by my unexpected manoeuvre, stumbles backwards into me and we both fall through the manhole into the stinking darkness below.

'Not again,' I groan as I struggle to my feet in the filth. Two visits to the sewers on one case seems excessive.

'Let's go.'

I bundle up the Cloth as quickly as I can and we head

off, while up above there is shouting and confusion.

I don't know where we are. I've never been in this part of the sewers before, so I let Hanama lead. She carries a small lantern of cunning design which lights our way.

I'm not sure why I'm following her. I don't think we're allies. At least she's taking me away from Glixius. I solemnly swear to myself that if I survive this night then I will make every sacrifice, including beer, to buy myself a new spell protection charm. They're hideously expensive but I can't go running scared from Sorcerers all the time, not in my line of work.

'Where are we going?'

'Exit on the shore,' replies Hanama, who seems entirely at home down in the sewers.

'Keep a look out for alligators,' I pant to Makri.

'I will,' she replies, and even she seems slightly worried by the prospect. We make good time. The level of sewage is low due to the long spell of hot weather. Water in Turai's aqueducts has already started to run short. Hanama suddenly comes to a halt.

'We're close to the exit.'

With that she abruptly douses her lamp. Before I realise what she's up to she grabs the Cloth and tries to yank it from me. I hold on grimly and in consequence we both fall over and start rolling around in the filth, struggling for the Cloth. I'd say she was a more skilful close-combat fighter, but I have a weight advantage.

'Let go!' hisses Hanama. We struggle some more, till my senses again pick up an ominous warning.

'Glixius,' I yell. 'Magic coming.'

'What's that noise?' calls Makri, as a huge roaring starts reverberating through the tunnels.

'It sounds like a flood.'

'It can't be, it's summer.'

Suddenly and terrifyingly a huge wave of water surges through the tunnel, carrying us off with it. I'm buffeted and dragged along, unable to breath as the flood water carries us before it like rats. My last conscious thought is to curse Glixius Dragon Killer for unleashing such a thing. The man is completely heartless. I didn't even know there was a flood water spell. Eventually I pass out, with visions of my past life flickering before my eyes.

I drift back to consciousness somewhere on the sea shore, beached like a whale. I cough and retch about ten gallons of water out of my lungs and rise unsteadily to my knees. It's very dark and I can just make out the figure of Makri lying close by. As I struggle towards her she opens her eyes and turns on her side to spew out the water she's swallowed.

'Still alive?'

'Just about,' mutters Makri, clambering to her feet. She's relieved to find she still has both her swords. She brought them with her from the Orcish gladiator pits, and they're fine weapons. Orcs might be hated the world over, but they make a fine blade. Then I notice something wrapped around my fingers. A strip of Red Cloth, ripped from the main roll. I stare at it glumly. I doubt if anyone will pay me a reward of six hundred gurans for this miserable fragment. I curse, and stuff it in my pocket. Hanama must have kept hold of the rest. As usual, she has now disappeared. With the Cloth. I curse.

'I can't shake that damned woman off. She's sharp as an Elf's ear at this investigating business. How the hell did she know to come to the church?'

I haul myself up the rocky beach. I come to a halt, surprised. Lying prostrate beside a pool is the small figure of Hanama. As we approach she rolls over and groans. Makri hurries and kneels down beside her.

'Someone's slugged her.'

The Assassin has a nasty wound on the back of her head. She comes round at the sound of our voices. Makri cradles her head and drips a little water from her flask into her mouth.

'Thanks, Makri,' says the Assassin. She struggles to her feet.

'What happened?'

'Someone hit me from behind. I was still spewing up water from the flood—'

'So where's the Cloth?' I demand.

Hanama stares coolly at me, and turns on her heel. She makes her way up the beach, unsteadily. I stare after her, but don't bother pursuing her. She wouldn't answer questions from me if her life depended on it.

Two of the three moons are visible in the sky. Light from them glimmers on a rock about the size of my fist. I reach down and find it is sticky with still damp blood. Whoever hit the Assassin didn't bother with anything fancy. I slip the rock into my pocket.

Makri and I reach the patch of waste ground that leads into the warehouses beside the harbour. Steam rises from my clothes in the heat of the night. At least the flood water washed off the sewage. We walk past a warehouse and turn the corner and there, right in front of us, is Glixius Dragon Killer. He looks bedraggled, as if he might have been caught up in his own flood.

'You—' he begins, and starts to raise his voice for a spell.

Nothing happens. His spells have run out. I smile.

'Too bad, Glixius,' I say, and punch him in the face as hard as I can It's a good punch. There's a lot of feeling behind it, and a lot of weight. He goes down in a heap and stays there.

'Nice punch,' says Makri, admiringly.

'Thank you.'

After all this magic, there's something very pleasing about a good punch.

We walk on. Part one of tonight's mission is a failure. Let's hope the next part goes better. We have an appointment with Sarin the Merciless but we don't get far. Before we reach Quintessence Street three landuses hurtle up and screech to a halt beside us. Pontifexes, twelve of them, leap out and surround us. At least, they're wearing priestly garments, but as they're carrying swords and look like they know how to use them, I guess they belong to a fairly specialised division of the Church.

'Bishop Gzekius would like to see you.'

Makri's hands go to her swords. I shake my head.

'Fine. I'll be delighted to see the Bishop.'

We climb in and the landuses take us off through the still dark streets of the city.

The Head of the Church in Turai is Archbishop Xerius, who has four equally ranked Bishops under him. Gzekius's parish includes Twelve Seas but he doesn't live there of course. He lives in a very large villa up in Thamlin, where he gets his relief from ministering to the poor by sitting by his swimming pool eating delicacies from his own private fish ponds.

Gzekius is a large, powerful man, around fifty with thick grey hair. Ambitious too, though he conceals it fairly well under his normally placid exterior. I say normally, because when we are led in he looks far from peaceful. In fact he's close to exploding and wastes no time in threatening me with arrest, excommunication and a lengthy visit to the prison galleys.

I regard him coolly while he thunders on about the desecration of churches and the general disgraceful state of the citizenry in Turai, particularly me. 'It's all very well threatening me, Bishop,' I say, when I can get a word in. 'But I wouldn't say you're in too strong a position yourself. I doubt that the King will be very amused to hear that you stole the Cloth in the first place. Illegal for anyone but the King to have it, remember. And of course there's also the matter of Attilan. Your man stole the spell from the garden. Had he murdered the diplomat before I got there?'

'How dare you accuse the True Church of murder!' fumes the Bishop.

'Not forgetting stealing a spell, and putting the King's dragon to sleep then hacking it to death. I'd say you might be joining me on the prison ship.'

I'd hoped to shake the Bishop with this. He doesn't look shaken, but he does calm down a little.

'Neither myself nor the Church had any involvement in the theft of the Cloth.' He claims that he has no idea how the Cloth came to be in Derlex's church. 'Do you seriously expect anyone to believe that one Pontifex stole a dragon sleep spell from a Niojan diplomat while another helped cut the cloth out of the dragon?'

'Yes.'

'They won't. Not when the accusation comes from a man like you, Thraxas,' he says dismissively.

'I might not be able to persuade the King or the Consul, Bishop Gzekius, though I'll have a good try. But I'll sure as hell persuade Praetor Cicerius. And remember, it wasn't just me that saw you and Derlex with the Elvish Cloth. So did an Assassin, the Brotherhood and the Society of Friends. And the Orcish Ambassadors must know you had it as well, because they sent their Orcs to recover it. That's a whole host of witnesses. None of them good witnesses I grant you, but more than enough to persuade the population that you've been up to something. A very juicy story for the *Chronicle*. Very poor publicity for the Church, Bishop, particularly at a time when Senator Lodius is on the rampage. He doesn't like you at all. What was it he called you last week? "Bloodsucking parasites on the poor", I believe.'

We face each other in silence for a while. I help myself to a little wine. Makri stands mutely in a corner, uncomfortable in these surroundings.

'I don't know why you wanted the Cloth. Maybe you just needed some cash. But I think you might have been looking to make a magic-proof room for yourself. You're an ambitious man, Bishop Gzekius. The Archbishopric comes up for grabs soon. You are not favourite for the job, but everyone knows you want it. So it's going to take some serious plotting on your part to land it. The other Bishops in Turai wouldn't like it at all if you had a magic-proof room. Far too much of an advantage in plotting. So they'll believe my story anyway.'

The Bishop raises his eyebrows slightly, which seems to signify that I've got through to him. He dismisses his attendants from the room. I help myself to some more wine. Tastes like a fine vintage.

'Where is the Cloth now?' he demands, when we're alone.

I tell him truthfully that I don't know.

'Disappeared down a sewer and it's probably not coming back. Which is bad for me, as I was meant to be finding it. But that's not my main problem. I'm meant to be clearing the Princess's name. That's what I've been hired to do. The rest doesn't bother me too much. Help me sort that one out and the whole sordid story will never pass my lips.'

Bishop Gzekius sips his own wine, savouring it. 'Are you telling me that you were not after the Cloth for yourself, Investigator?'

I shake my head. 'Just doing the work I was hired for.'

The Bishop looks at me for a long time. He's puzzled by the thought that I might be honest. He transfers his gaze to Makri. He's wondering how far he can trust us.

'I have heard, Thraxas, that you do perform the job you are paid for. In an honest fashion. Perhaps I can trust you to keep your word. It would, in some ways, be easier than having you killed.'

We stare at each other. It floats through my mind that Pontifex Derlex must have given him a reasonable report of my character, which comes as a surprise.

'And how would you suggest I help clear the Princess's name?'

I shrug. 'Call in some favours at the Palace. From what I hear, the King owes you a few. The Cloth's gone now, it doesn't do you or the Church any good to have a major royal scandal.'

The Bishop stares at me for a while longer. 'I do have influence,' he says, finally. 'Enough to sway the King, possibly. And enough to make your life in Twelve Seas short and full of incident. So be sure never to trouble me again.'

He dismisses us from his presence.

'What did that mean?' asks Makri, as we find ourselves again out in the warm night-time streets.

'I think it means he'll help the Princess. And give me hell if our paths ever cross again. Well, that'll do for now.'

I glance up at the stars.

'About an hour till we're due to meet Sarin. We've just got time to go and see Astrath Triple Moon. It's high time I had some proper sorcerous help on all this. Someone slugged Hanama and took the Cloth and I want to know who. Also I wonder if he might locate Sarin. Tas of the Eastern Lightning couldn't find her but, whatever means she was using to hide, she might be out in the open now. If I knew where she was I might be able to take her by surprise and get the letter back for free. No point wasting thousands of Cicerius's gurans if we don't have to.'

I glance at Makri. 'Incidentally, when did you and Hanama become friends?'

'What? We're not friends.'

'Oh yeah? The way you cradled her head when we found her unconscious seemed pretty friendly to me. And she said, "Thanks, Makri," when you gave her water. That's friendly for an Assassin.'

Makri snorts dismissively. 'So? She'd been hit on the head. You're rambling, Thraxas. I only met her one time, when she attacked you in your room.'

I'm suspicious about this, but I let it lie, and we hurry down to visit Astrath Triple Moon. It's still the middle of the night. The streets are quiet, except for a few bakery workers on their way to light the ovens for tomorrow's bread.

Our visit to Astrath is unproductive. He doesn't actually mind too much that I wake him in the middle of the night, but when I ask him if he can locate Sarin he draws a blank. Likewise for the six sacks of dwa.

'She must have left the city.'

'Impossible. She's due to meet us at the Stadium Superbius in half an hour.'

The Sorcerer shrugs and asks if I've anything else he can look at. I still have the fragment of the Red Elvish Cloth but of course he can learn nothing from that. By now I am fairly sick of Red Elvish Cloth. The stuff is nothing but trouble. I hand him the rock I've been carrying, the one that was used to club Hanama, and ask him if he can learn anything from it.

'Take me a while, Thraxas. It's always difficult getting information from rocks. Auras cling to them very tenuously, if at all.'

I tell him to do his best, and meanwhile ask if he can lend us his landus.

'You can't ride in the city at night.'

'I have senatorial privilege.'

'Really?'

'No. But I'm working for Cicerius, so I can pretend. And we're late.'

'So which one of us is the Senator?' enquires Makri, as we thunder off in the carriage.

Makri knows full well that women can't be Senators. I'm starting to think she's going to too many of those meetings.

CHAPTER
TWENTY-SIX

In the centre of the town Civil Guards are still out in force because of the tension that hangs over the city. Wild rumours abound about cancelled elections, planned coups, bribery and assassination. It's even whispered that the Royal Family has been buying drugs from the Orcs and selling them to the population.

The Guards challenge us. 'Urgent business for Praetor Cicerius,' I roar, and gallop on towards the Stadium. I have with me a bag of gold from Cicerius and instructions to bid as high as is necessary to obtain the Prince's letter of credit.

The Stadium Superbius is situated just inside the city walls, over on the east side of town. It's an enormous stone amphitheatre, built by King Varquius a hundred years or so ago, and it's a very important place. It's the setting for circuses, theatrical performances, religious ceremonies, gladiatorial shows and, cause of my recent misfortune, the chariot races. I love the chariot races. Twice a week during the racing season the amphitheatre is packed full of race-goers from every stratum of Turanian society. Praetors, Prefects, Senators, priests, society ladies, Sorcerers, high-ranking guild officials: all mingle with the huge mass of proletarian Turanians there to enjoy a day out and maybe pick up a little money on the side. Prince Frisen-Akan is an enthusiastic race-goer with his own stable of chariots. Even the King sometimes attends. Naturally, the Stadium Superbius also attracts a swarm of petty criminals, and most of the bookmakers are controlled by the Brotherhood or the Society of Friends.

We dismount from the landus and stride into the giant, dark building. Makri has a torch with her. She lights it, casting weird shadows on to the old stone walls from the statues of famous gladiators and charioteers of the past. No one is in sight.

I take out the strip of Red Elvish Cloth I wrenched from Hanama's hands in the sewer, and rip it in two.

'Tie this round your neck.'

Makri looks perplexed.

'If Sarin's here then so is her associate Glixius Dragon Killer. This strip of cloth will act as a spell protection charm.'

'Are you sure?'

'Not sure at all. But it might.'

We round the Triumphal Arch through which the victors parade at the end of the games. In front of us, in the shadows, a figure lies prostrate on the ground. We draw our swords and advance carefully. Makri kneels down.

'It's Sarin,' she hisses. 'She's been clubbed on the back of the head.'

First Hanama and now Sarin. Someone's making my life easier. I glance around. No one's in sight, but down by the wall there is a small pile of dull white powder. I reach down, poke my finger in it and taste.

'Dwa. Looks like Sarin had the sacks with her and someone seized them.'

Makri also pokes her finger in the powder and tastes it. This does not seem strictly necessary to me but I let it pass.

I kneel down and start searching Sarin. 'She might still have the letter. No point paying for it if we don't have to.'

Sarin has been clubbed quite viciously and I'd swear she'll be out for a long time but to my surprise she suddenly opens her eyes. To my further surprise she yanks my long braid in a very painful manner and sends me tumbling away in the dust. She leaps to her feet. Despite her recent lapse from conciousness and the ugly wound on her head, she faces me in a fighting crouch.

'Lost your crossbow?' I jeer, and charge in, aiming a blow of my own. A cunning street fighter, I feint with my left and land her with my right. At least that's the theory. Sarin avoids both blows and kicks me in the ribs, sending me hurtling backwards. I pick myself up, fairly puzzled at this turn of events. I hurtle in again, figuring to overpower her with my weight, but Sarin performs some fancy move which I don't exactly follow, except I end up on the ground again. I get pretty mad because I notice out the corner of my eye that Makri, instead of leaping in to help like she should, is actually laughing. I draw my sword. Sarin takes out a small knife. We circle each other. I can't find an opening. I can't understand it at all. I wasn't lying when I said I'd run her out of town before. How the hell she has returned as a hardened warrior is beyond me.

We exchange a few blows. I'm starting to get short of breath. I've been fighting and running around to excess in the last twenty-four hours and I don't seem to have

eaten or slept. The heat is getting to me. I lunge at Sarin
and she parries again and kicks my legs from under me,
so I fall very heavily to the ground. I struggle up again
and turn my head towards Makri.

'Will you stop standing there like a eunuch in a
brothel and give a man some help?'

'Just giving you a chance, Thraxas. You told me you'd
be down on her like a bad spell if she showed her face
again.'

I glare at Makri then make another assault on Sarin.
I'll show her who's number one chariot round here. She
parries my sword with her small knife then hits me so
hard with the flat of her hand that I'm sent spinning into
the wall where I once more slump to the ground.

Before Sarin can follow up, Makri decides she's had
enough laughs for one day and appears above me with
her sword drawn.

She confronts Sarin. 'Thraxas tells me you can't fight.'

I clamber painfully to my feet. 'Well, she didn't used to
be able to.'

'Three years in the warrior monastery at Kvalir,' says
Sarin, and almost smiles.

'I take it you weren't studying religion,' I say, grateful
for the chance to catch my breath.

'No. Just fighting. I used to find it annoying the way
people could defeat me. No one defeats me now.'

'You weren't looking too good when we found you.'

'Someone crept up behind me.' Sarin the Merciless
frowns, and looks a little puzzled. 'Normally no one
could do that.'

'Maybe your pal Glixius Dragon Killer decided he
didn't want you around any more.'

She shakes her head. 'Glixius is no longer my associate. Horm and Glixius double-crossed me. After I cleared the way for them with my crossbow, they tried to edge me out of the operation. They didn't like sharing their profits with a third party. Particularly a woman.'

She shrugs. 'So much the worse for them. I outsmarted them. And it was not Glixius who clubbed me. He wouldn't be capable.'

She casts her eyes around, and looks troubled. 'My horse has gone. And the dwa.' She reaches into her tunic and produces the Prince's letter. 'But I still have this. And it will cost you ten thousand gurans. Unless you would like to try and take it off me?'

I'd as soon not. I remain silent.

'To business,' she says.

'I believe that letter is mine,' comes a voice.

A tall figure in a rainbow cloak strides out of the darkness. It's Glixius Dragon Killer. He glowers at me with hatred in his eyes.

'I presume we are seeking the same item,' he says.

I grunt in reply.

'You are wasting your time, Thraxas. The letter is mine.'

'You seem to be having trouble holding on to it.'

'I was not expecting such treachery from Sarin the Merciless.'

I turn to Sarin. 'So what are you going to do now? I doubt if your warrior monk training is going to enable you to fend off me, Makri and Glixius.'

Sarin sneers. I haven't impressed her.

'As representatives of the honourable politicians in this city, you make a sorry pair. An obese, drunken

Investigator and a treacherous criminal Sorcerer.' She holds up the letter. 'For blackmailing a Prince. The opening price is ten thousand gurans. Who'd like to make an offer?'

Glixius Dragon Killer has no intention of bidding. He raises his hand to fire a spell at her. Seconds later he is tossed to the ground and lies stunned. His spell has rebounded on him. Another rainbow-clad figure floats gently down from the top of the arch.

'Who's that?' says Makri.

'Tas of the Eastern Lightning,' I reply. 'Looks like Palace Security are getting in on the act at last.'

I'm expecting Tas to wrest the letter from Sarin and possibly send her crashing into a wall with a spell for good measure. What he actually does is stroll over and kiss her lightly on the cheek. Makri and I look on in amazement as she kisses him back.

'No wonder he said he couldn't find her. They're in league now.'

'Indeed we are,' booms Tas, a tall man with long brown hair tumbling down over his rainbow cloak.

'What's the matter with these Sorcerers in Turai?' I snarl, cursing them all. 'If they're not dwa addicts or drunks, then they're psychotic criminals.'

'Lucky you never finished your studies,' whispers Makri, eyeing the pair warily. 'Is Tas more powerful than you?'

'Like a tiger compared to a rat. Try not to upset him. Remember what happened to Mirius Eagle Rider.'

'Do I hear a bid?' calls Sarin the Merciless.

I offer her the ten thousand gurans. Glixius Dragon Killer hauls himself to his feet and swears a savage oath.

He fires up another spell and Tas bounces it right back, sending Glixius thudding to the ground again. It's a sight I enjoy. I'd kick him while he's down but I haven't the time.

'It seems you are the only bidder, Thraxas,' says Sarin. 'Very well, ten thousand gurans to you.'

Sarin holds out the letter. I hold out the bag of gold. The transaction is interrupted by a bolt of lightning which sears into the ground between us, sending everyone flying. I land on my back, staring stupidly at the sky. Just discernible in the darkness is the vast shape of a war dragon, something not seen this far west since the war ended fifteen years ago. Its nostrils are red with fire and riding atop the beast is the crazed figure of Horm the Dead, long black hair and feather jewellery flying in the wind. His shrill voice cuts through the night.

'The letter is rightfully mine, I believe.'

Tas of the Eastern Lightning climbs calmly to his feet. 'Not yours, Horm the Dead.'

With that Tas unleashes a spell that sends the dragon spinning through the sky, screaming with rage and bafflement.

'Wow,' says Makri.

We're impressed. Horm the Dead and a war dragon obviously hold no terrors for Tas of the Eastern Lightning. Horm regains control and flies back overhead.

'Save your energy, Tas of the Eastern Lightning,' shouts Horm. 'I haven't come for the letter, or the gold, or to fight with you, though one day I will kill you at my leisure.'

'At your leisure,' shouts Tas. 'Then why have you come?'

'To destroy your city, and all the Humans in it who I

have found so annoying of late. Humans such as
yourself, Thraxas.'

Horm the Dead starts to intone a spell. A very long
spell, in Orcish, never before heard in the world. He
completes his incantation, waves us a mocking farewell,
then wheels his dragon up and away into the night. We
all stare at each other. Nothing seems to be happening.

'What was that all about?'

Tas of the Eastern Lightning looks very grim. He takes
Sarin's hand. 'Get the gold. It's time to go. That was the
city-devouring spell. The Eight-Mile Terror. Horm has
remade it. Madness will now grip the population. Turai is
going to be destroyed.'

I should know better than to aggravate these mad
half-Orc Sorcerers. You never know when they might
come and destroy your city.

'I don't feel anything,' protests Sarin.

'You're wearing a protective necklace,' says Tas. 'So
am I. But the population isn't.'

Outside a low murmuring is growing in intensity. We
run from the Stadium Superbius and are confronted
with the terrible sight of the city starting to burn. Yellow
flames leap into the sky to meet the first rays of dawn.
Sarin holds out the letter.

'The gold,' she snaps.

I make the transaction, though what use it'll be once
Turai succumbs to the flames of madness I don't know.
Glixius Dragon Killer runs up behind me and tries to
snatch the letter out of my hand. Sarin the Merciless
executes a faultless kick to his head, worthy indeed of a
trained warrior monk, and Glixius slumps unconscious
to the ground.

'A bad mistake to double-cross me,' she mutters. She takes out a knife and bends over him. I think she's going to finish him off but instead, with a malicious grin, she slits his protective charm and takes it from his neck.

'Happy awakenings,' she says, putting her arm round Tas's waist. Tas mutters a spell and they rise into the air.

'You can't just leave Turai to be destroyed!'

'I believe Lisutaris, Mistress of the Sky, was working on a counterspell to Horm's Eight-Mile Terror,' calls Tas, now high above us. 'She might be able to save you all, if she can stay awake long enough.'

They disappear into the blackness.

'Why wouldn't Lisutaris, Mistress of the Sky, be able to stay awake?'

'She's always stoned. Smokes her thazis through a big water pipe.'

Glixius stirs.

'We better get out of here.'

We run. Behind us Glixius screams like a maniac and starts bellowing out spell after spell, far more than he could possibly retain in his memory in normal circumstances. Statues start falling from plinths and walls explode in flame as the now insane sorcerer vents his wrath on the world.

'That Sarin is a mean woman!' I gasp, as we dive for the safety of the nearest buildings. 'I don't give much for Tas's chances once he's outlived his usefulness.'

All of a sudden we're surrounded by demented citizens waving clubs and swords and attacking anything that moves. An old woman with a stick charges at Makri. Makri boots her out the way but is obliged to gut a huge northern mercenary who flies at her with a battle axe.

We flee into an alleyway and leap the wall at the end, seeking safety, though nowhere is safe. Between us and every city gate is a crowd driven mad by Horm the Dead's evil spell.

A hand appears from nowhere and grabs Makri. She disappears with a yelp into a doorway. I plunge after her and find her in the grip of a small dark figure. It's Hanama, Master Assassin.

'Oh God, not a mad Assassin,' I cry, and leap at her throat. Hanama side-steps neatly and I thump against the wall.

'Not a mad Assassin,' says Hanama coolly, and fingers her own protective necklace, made from the same Red Elvish Cloth as mine.

I don't know if this meeting is a coincidence or if Hanama has been following us. With the city starting to self-destruct there is no time to think about it.

The Assassin scans the crowd with distaste. 'My guild dislikes too much social unrest,' she says. 'Some discontent is good for business, but too much always spoils things.'

'True, Hanama. No one needs Assassins when everyone's killing everyone else anyway. I guess the investigating business will go downhill as well.'

'We'd better try and reach Lisutaris' house,' says Makri, and explains to Hanama that the Sorcerer may have a countermanding spell to the Eight-Mile Terror. Hanama agrees. I look at her with suspicion. Her behaviour of late has been strange, out of character for an Assassin. They usually keep themselves to themselves, apart from when they're killing people.

I have no great hopes of Lisutaris being able to end the

riot but I don't have any better idea. Besides, it's possible that the Sorcerers up in Truth is Beauty Lane will be able to hold off the maddened crowds so it seems as good a destination as any. I can't say I'm pleased to throw in my lot with an Assassin though, and I tell her to depart.

Twenty or so soldiers, fully armed and fully maddened, charge up the street towards us. We flee, and I find myself keeping company with Hanama anyway, much against my will.

Unfortunately, Truth is Beauty Lane is a popular destination for the crazed inhabitants of the city. Even in their madness they see that it will be a fine place to burn. Everyone has gone violently insane. Apart from the Royal Family, only Sorcerers, senior officials and a few wealthy merchants have protective necklaces, and I wouldn't give much for their chances against the demented mob.

Makri and Hanama's fighting skills and my enormous body weight get us close. The resident Sorcerers are making a desperate effort to keep the crazed citizens at bay. The air crackles with magical energy as the barrier they've erected is subjected to a continual barrage of flaming torches and missiles. Not all of the Sorcerers in Truth is Beauty Lane are as powerful as Tas of the Eastern Lightning or Harmon Half Elf. Many of them are little better than astrologers, with few more resources than myself, and the effort is starting to tell on them. Gorsius Starfinder, and Old Hasius the Brilliant, Chief Sorcerer at the Abode of Justice, both powerful Sorcerers, stand firmly in the street repelling all comers, but several of their companions are starting to retreat, forced back by the weight of incoming missiles. A few firebrands penetrate the magical barrier and the houses at the end of the street start to burn. Of Lisutaris, Mistress of the Sky, there is no sign.

The crowd are fully occupied with the attack and make no attempt to prevent us drawing near. When we reach the end of the street I bellow at Gorsius Starfinder at the top of my voice, straining to make myself heard above the roar of the mob. Gorsius hears me. He stares at me dubiously. I hold up my protective necklace, screaming for him to let me in. He motions with his staff. The barrier flickers. Hanama, Makri and I plunge through.

'Bad place to come for refuge,' gasps Gorsius Starfinder, who's standing flinging spells in his underwear, having not even had time to don his rainbow cloak. 'We can't hold them off much longer.'

'Where's Lisutaris?'

'Stoned, I expect,' says Gorsius, ducking as a rock flies overhead.

'Tas of the Eastern Lightning told me she was working on a counterspell to the Eight-Mile Terror.'

'The Eight-Mile Terror?' screams Gorsius. 'Is that what has caused this?'

'What did you think it was? Something in the water?'

Gorsius groans. 'Then there is no chance of it ending. Where is Tas? We need his help.'

'He's not coming, I'm afraid.'

In the distance flames are rising from the Imperial Palace. Another rock penetrates the barrier. Gorsius Starfinder crumples to the ground. His Apprentice runs up and drags him to safety but the Sorcerers are now harder pressed than ever. Some of the junior ones who've never been to war are losing their nerve. We sprint up the road to Lisutaris' mansion. Around it lie the bodies of her servants, subdued in their madness by the Sorcerers. The door is locked.

'The crowd just advanced,' says Makri.

I charge like an elephant and the door splinters. Hanama, fleetest of foot, is the first to find the Mistress of the Sky, Sorcerer of vast power, and hopeless thazis abuser. She's lying beside her water pipe with a faraway look on her face. The room is thick with smoke, thicker than the Avenging Axe after an all-night celebration. The woman really does smoke far too much of this stuff. Once more I curse the degeneracy of our Palace Sorcerers.

'Try and rouse her, Makri. I'll look for the spell.'

Makri starts shaking Lisutaris, while Hanama and I tear the house apart looking for the counterspell to the Eight-Mile Terror. From outside the roar of the crowd intensifies as more and more of the demented citizens break through the Sorcerers' barrier.

As I plunge into Lisutaris' workroom a crazed servant appears from somewhere waving a carving knife. I dodge the strike and slug him. He's too mad to feel it and comes at me again so I trip him up and break a chair over his head. If we survive Lisutaris can patch him up later. I start rummaging through the Sorcerer's books.

'Is this it?' asks Hanama, appearing with a freshly written parchment. I study it quickly.

'Afraid not, this is a spell for making thazis plants grow quicker.' Hanama tosses it away in disgust and we carry on searching. A rock crashes through the window. The crowd are closing in. Gorsius Starfinder and his

Apprentice stumble in through a back door, dragging Old Hasius the Brilliant with them. All three are cut and bleeding.

'The crowd's breaking through!'

Hasius the Brilliant is reputed to be a hundred and ten years old. He'll be lucky to reach a hundred and eleven if the counterspell doesn't turn up soon. I drag open another drawer, and uncover various newly worked parchments, which I scan frantically.

'Yes!' I scream in triumph. 'A counterspell to the Eight-Mile Terror!'

Gorsius hobbles over to study it with me. As he reads through it quickly, he wipes blood from his face. More rocks crash through the windows. His face falls.

'She hasn't finished it.'

I quit the room immediately and tell Makri to stop trying to revive Lisutaris, Mistress of the Sky.

'She hasn't finished the spell. There's nothing to do now but get out of here before the whole city goes up in flames.'

'Well, so much for civilisation,' says Makri, and makes to leave with me.

'Where are you going?' demands Gorsius Starfinder, appearing beside us.

'Anywhere. We're going to fight our way out before the city burns.'

'You can't just run away,' protests the Sorcerer.

'Only thing to do,' says Makri, matter-of-factly. 'We can't fight the whole population.'

'Just buy us some time. Lisutaris can complete the spell.'

Before I can reply the door crashes open and there

stands Glixius Dragon Killer with madness in his eyes.

'Death to all Sorcerers!' he screams.

He leaps towards me, arms raised. I hope my spell protector is strong enough to resist his insane sorcery.

I don't get the chance to find out because instead of casting a spell Glixius punches me full in the face and I tumble to the floor. He screams with laughter.

'I enjoyed that,' he says, and draws his sword.

Makri leaps in front to protect me and engages Glixius in combat. At that moment a horde of deranged rioters burst into the house waving swords and flaming torches. Makri and I flee the room, dragging Gorsius Starfinder and Lisutaris with us. We run back to the workroom where we find Hasius the Brilliant slumped unconscious and Hanama expelling two intruders from the back door.

We're surrounded. We barricade the doors with furniture, and look at each other, wondering what to do. Lisutaris, Mistress of the Sky, moans, and shows signs of coming round. The mad crowd hammer on the door and there's the sound of axes breaking it down.

'Can't all you Sorcerers do something?' demands Makri.

We can't. No one has any spells left. Mine went long ago and the collective power of all the others was dissipated in holding the crowd back in the street outside. We have no more power than anyone else. Less, given the condition of Hasius, Gorsius and Lisutaris. Smoke starts to creep under the door. The rioters have set the house on fire.

CHAPTER
TWENTY-SEVEN

Somebody is screaming, 'Put the fire out, put the fire out!'

It's me. No one puts the fire out.

I don't believe it. Here I am, surrounded by Turai's most powerful Sorcerers, and I'm going to die in a house fire.

'Doesn't anyone have even one spell left?'

Gorsius Starfinder shakes his head. His Apprentice looks blank. Hasius the Brilliant is unconscious. Lisutaris, Mistress of the Sky, is still stoned. The smoke gets thicker. Flames lick under the door. Makri and Hanama try to wrench the door open but it now seems to be barricaded from the outside.

I lose my temper completely. I grab Lisutaris, haul her to her feet and give her a slap which nearly takes her head off. She opens her eyes, and grins stupidly.

'Hello!' I scream. 'Anybody there? Listen good. We're about to burn to death. No one else has any power left so it's up to you. Put the fire out.'

'What?'

'PUT THE FIRE OUT!'

'No need to shout,' says Lisutaris, showing some signs of coming back to reality. She waves her hand. The fire goes out.

'I'm really hungry,' she says.

I beat the door down with a few mighty blows. Lisutaris' spell has ejected the rioters from the house but they are screaming outside, regrouping for another attack. I'm getting out of here. Unfortunately an even larger crowd of maniacs, including several heavily armed soldiers, now surrounds the house, occupying the Praetor's gardens like an invading army. All of a sudden a fancy landus careers into view. The driver is struggling desperately to control the horse as all around missiles fly and flames spurt into the sky.

The carriage thunders through an ornamental hedge and over some beds of flowers before scything its way through the crowd. Whoever is in it seems to be deliberately heading our way.

'Nice driving,' mutters Makri, as the carriage veers round some trees at a furious pace. The driver is hunched down low, trying to avoid the rocks hurled by the rabid mob. It almost makes it to the house but comes shuddering to a halt when the front wheels get stuck in an ornamental pond.

'It's the Princess!'

'She's picked a poor time for a jail break.'

Du-Akai, showing more spirit than I would have given her credit for, leaps from the driver's pillion, fends off an attacker and dashes towards us, crowd in pursuit. She makes it to the front door and we haul her in. She collapses on the floor, panting for breath. Unfortunately for her, her sanctuary is likely to be brief. Maddened by her appearance the crowd charge the house and start removing the door frame. Any second now they'll be pouring through. I groan, and turn quickly to Lisutaris.

'Finish your counterspell and make it quick!' I tell her, then wearily get back to the task of preserving my life against the mob. Hanama and Makri join me at the door and we hold them off the best we can. Even in their maniacal state, the sight of our three blades is enough to deter some of the rabble, but the soldiers seem to relish the opportunity for combat and fly at us like we are hostile Orcs. It's a grim battle, and the fact that we're being forced to slay innocent people makes it worse. Horm the Dead has certainly wreaked a terrible revenge. Makri should never have stuck him with that throwing star.

I've just dispatched an opponent when Lisutaris, Mistress of the Sky, shouts at us from behind. 'What's the Orcish for "peace"?'

I'm baffled by this interruption.

'What are you talking about?' I scream.

'I have to translate my counterspell into Orcish to make it work. My Orcish isn't very good. What's their word for "peace"?'

'*Vazey*,' yells Makri, kicking an opponent away from her.

We carry on fighting.

'What's the Orcish for "Harmonious Conjunction"?'

This takes Makri a few minutes, which is not surprising as she's locked in combat with a huge soldier carrying a twin-bladed axe.

'*Tenasata zadad*, I think!' she screams back after dispatching him.

Bodies are now everywhere but the attackers don't let up. Their madness seems to be intensifying and smoke is starting to drift into the room from the houses burning in the street. I've got a serious cut on my face and another on my shoulder and I notice that Hanama isn't moving too well and seems to be wounded in the leg.

'What's the Orcish for "All men shall be brothers"?'

'For God's sake, Makri, go back there and translate her damned spell. Me and Hanama will hold them off.'

Makri sees the wisdom of this and hurries back leaving myself and the Assassin to fight on. In my vainer moments I've been known to claim to be the best street fighter in the city. This is an exaggeration, but I am good at it. So is Hanama. I wonder about the incongruity of fighting shoulder to shoulder with a heartless Assassin, but I don't wonder for long because a truly frightening opponent now leaps at me. He's one of the largest men I've ever seen and he's carrying an axe the size of a door. He attacks me with a ferocity that drives me backwards, and I find it almost impossible to block his axe. He's extremely fierce and strong and I'm too weary to fight much longer. I lunge at him and stick my sword in his shoulder, but he's madder than a mad Sorcerer and doesn't even feel it. His axe crashes on to my hastily raised blade and I'm forced to my knees. He chops at me again and my arm goes numb. I drop my sword. He slashes at my throat.

His blade stops right at my skin and he tumbles to the ground with Hanama's knife sticking in his back. I gasp out a thank you and haul myself to my feet, ready to meet the next wave of attackers. Behind me I can hear Makri, Lisutaris and the other Sorcerers bandying around Orcish and Elvish terms as they try to complete the counterspell.

Hanama's wounded leg gives way and she sinks to one

knee, heavily pressed. Again showing some spirit, the Princess runs forward and clubs an opponent to the ground. I'm gripped with sudden fury about being forced to make my death stand in such a useless manner. I never figured I'd go out fighting a crowd of demented Turanian shopkeepers. I turn my head and bellow at the top of my voice.

'If you don't finish that spell, Lisutaris, I'll come and kill you myself before they get me!'

'Hold on,' she shouts in reply. 'Another minute.'

We hold on for another minute. As Lisutaris starts intoning the spell I go down under the weight of six attackers armed with clubs, and pass out of consciousness.

When I wake it's dark and quiet. Either I'm dead or the riot's stopped. A door opens, letting light into the room, and Makri enters. Her head is bandaged, but she seems healthy.

'What happened?'

'Lisutaris' counterspell worked. The whole city started to return to sanity about three hours ago. Just in time for you and Hanama. Good fighting, incidentally.'

'Thank you.'

I notice that I'm not feeling too bad, considering what I've been through.

'The Sorcerers patched you both up. After they'd seen to the Princess of course. All the rioters have departed to put out fires and lick their wounds. Half the city's been burned but the Sorcerers that are left seem to have it under control now, And the Civil Guard is out in force.

'Where's Hanama?'

'Next door. It took the Sorcerers a long time to heal her wounds.'

'Should have let her die.'

Makri points out this is rather ungrateful of me. Without Hanama, the mad crowd would have overwhelmed us.

'Maybe. Maybe not. I figure I had things pretty well under control. Well, time to get back to work, I guess.'

'Is it?'

I nod.

'I've got the Prince's letter back and probably gathered up enough information about the dwa dealing to keep Cerius out of court. Not sure about the Princess though. We'll have to hope that Bishop Gzekius comes through on that one and persuades the authorities that she didn't kill the dragon. And then there's the Cloth . . . I've been doing a fair bit of thinking about that . . . let's go and see Hanama.'

Makri declines. She's keen to get back to the Avenging Axe and check on things there. She's concerned that someone might have made off with the funds she's been collecting for the Association of Gentlewomen during the riot.

'What if my philosophy notes have been burned?'

Makri departs in a hurry, leaving me to seek out Hanama. The diminutive Assassin is not in the room next door, but I find her in the wine cellar sitting on the floor with a bottle in her hand. Her black clothes are in tatters after the fight but like me she seems in good shape after her healing.

'Well well,' I say. 'That makes two surprising discoveries about you in one day.'

'What?'

'Firstly, you can be sufficiently shaken by events to need a drink to calm you down.'

'I do not need a drink to calm me down,' says Hanama, coldly.

'Well, I do,' I say, selecting a bottle and opening it with the corkscrew I keep on my key ring, and sitting down beside her on the floor. 'We just fought off more maniacs than two Humans could reasonably be expected to cope with. A magnificent effort, though I say so myself. Anyone deserves a bottle of wine after that, even an Assassin, trained to be emotionless. Which brings me to my second discovery about you, Hanama. You're not emotionless.'

'And why do you say that?'

'You saved my life. I'm touched.'

'You shouldn't be. I merely saved you because I needed you at my side to fight off the mob.'

I don't pursue it. She's probably telling the truth. 'You know, Hanama, I seem to run across you a lot these days. I haven't worked out why that is yet. Still, I must say, for the number three in the Assassins Guild, you're not such a bad sort. A little distant, perhaps, but hey, for a woman who once scaled the sheer walls of Menhasat Castle in a snowstorm to assassinate Consul Pavius, you're not bad company. Is it true you once killed a Sorcerer, a Senator and an Orc Lord all in the same day?'

'The Assassins Guild does not discuss its work,' replies Hanama.

'Cheers,' I say, raising my bottle.

She raises her own a fraction, and we drink together. All around are wine racks stuffed with excellent vintages, though I can't see any beer. I finish one bottle and open another, selecting the finest I can find.

I don't bother asking Hanama why she has been after the Cloth as I know she will simply deny it. But I do express some surprise about finding her unconscious on the beach.

'Even though you'd just been half drowned in that sewer I'd have thought it was impossible for anyone to sneak up behind you.'

She looks faintly troubled. 'So would I. I swear I'd have sensed an attacker, half drowned or not.'

'Sorcery perhaps?'

She shakes her head. She didn't sense any sorcery and a

woman of her skills and training would have. I didn't pick up anything at the scene either. It remains a puzzling mystery. And a puzzling coincidence as well, now I think about it, because it seems very unlikely that anyone could sneak up behind Sarin the Merciless after the warrior monk training, yet they did. Obviously someone very good at sneaking is going around Turai clubbing people on the back of the head. Does that mean, I wonder, that the same person who took the Red Elvish Cloth from Hanama also took the dwa from Sarin? An interesting thought.

'There was something, but . . .'

I look at her inquisitively.

'I can't put my finger on it. But at the instant I was hit I thought I sensed . . . well I don't know . . . something not quite Human.'

'Like an Orc?'

She can't say. It was too fast and she was half drowned at the time. A dim memory rises inside me but disappears before I can identify it.

Hanama takes another drink then rises gracefully. It's time for her to get back to see how things are at Assassins Guild headquarters. As number three in the organisation, Hanama is important enough to wear a special protection charm, but that doesn't apply to all Assassins by any means. Must have made it interesting when they all went mad with the Eight-Mile Terror.

She leaves. I open another bottle of wine. The cellar is cool and it's the first time I've been comfortable in weeks. I find myself drifting off to sleep and it's an effort to rouse myself and get back to work.

'I guess it's better than rowing a slave galley,' I mutter, and haul myself to my feet.

CHAPTER
TWENTY-NINE

The Princess is wearing a new robe borrowed from Lisutaris and has brushed and plaited her golden hair. Her fancy arm bracelets are dented where she was struck by a rock, and she's lost an earring along the way, but all in all she looks not bad for a woman who had to fight her way through a riot. As I emerge from the cellar – to the well-deserved thanks and congratulations of the Sorcerers – she grabs an opportunity for a word. While not exactly apologising for her previous rudeness, she lets me know she thinks better of me now. I reply graciously. I can just about remember how from my days at the Palace.

The Sorcerers are recovering from the riot with a table full of delicacies and a generous selection of Lisutaris' wines, although I think Lisutaris herself is still a little on edge, probably because she feels that she is long overdue for a blast on her water pipe but doesn't actually want to smoke thazis while the Princess is still there. I don't expect the Princess would mind, what with the riot and everything, but a Sorcerer has to respect the forms of polite society if she wants to get on. Princess Du-Akai rises to leave. Lisutaris offers her a carriage and an escort back to the Palace, but it seems like the Princess has been waiting for my arrival because she declines the offer and elects to go with me. I grab a pastry off the Sorcerers' table and follow. Some servants haul the carriage out of the pond, fit a fresh horse on the front and I squeeze in behind her.

The sun is beating down even more strongly than yesterday. The ever present stals are wilting in the trees, what's left of them. After the coolness of Lisutaris' wine cellar it's hard to take.

'Hot as Orcish hell out here. Where exactly are you going, Princess? Back to captivity?'

She supposes so. When the riot broke out and she found herself trapped in a burning wing of the Palace she naturally decided that it would be a good idea to get out of there fast, but now it's all over it seems best to go back. She wouldn't get far if she fled for real. Too easily recognisable.

'I'll be locked up in my chambers again. Better than a prison cell, I suppose.'

We make our way slowly up the debris-strewn road. The elegant pavement tiles are cracked and soot-blackened. The trees, specially bred to stay green through the fierce summer, are broken and burned. Suddenly I spot two familiar figures emerging warily from the shattered front of another villa. It's Callis and Jaris, my Elvish clients. They're followed out by a couple of young and rather shaken-looking Sorcerers.

We stop and greet them. The Elves tell me that they were fortunate to be in Truth is Beauty Lane when the riot broke out, and they took shelter with the nearest Sorcerers. As Elves the Eight-Mile Terror did not affect them directly, but being trapped in the middle of thousands of mad Humans has shaken them badly.

They've had enough of city life. They're heading home and plan to take the next ship south out of the harbour at Twelve Seas. I'm displeased to have failed my clients but there's not a lot I can say. I came close to the Cloth but I didn't recover it. Clients are never impressed when you just come close, and neither am I. We bid each other farewell.

As we ride on the Princess expresses her disappointment at my failure.

I try to reassure her. 'I didn't get the Cloth back but I found out who gutted the dragon and removed it.'

I explain to her about Bishop Gzekius and the True Church. 'I can't exactly prove it in court but I have a fair amount of leverage over the Bishop and I reckon he'll do what's necessary to show you're innocent. If he does then it all stays quiet. Otherwise I'll have no choice but to give a full report on his recent activities for *The Renowned and Truthful Chronicle*. It loves a Church scandal.'

The Princess is grateful. She should be. Till I stepped in she was facing a lifetime in a mountain-top nunnery.

'Please also convey my gratitude to Makri for her efforts on my behalf.'

'I will.'

'This Cloth has proved to be very troublesome for Turai, Thraxas.'

'Anything floating round that's worth thirty thousand gurans is bound to be trouble.'

'Who ended up with it?'

The Palace is now in view. Smoke drifts above, but it's still in one piece, just about.

I admit I don't know who ended up with the Cloth.

'It was last seen in the hands of an Assassin but she

was clubbed by something not Human.'

'Not Human?'

'That's right. Which narrows it down I guess. Orcs, probably, or a half-Orc agent. Or . . .'

I feel some inspiration coming on. Right back at the start of the case, when I was being hauled away from Attilan's garden by the Guards. I sensed something there but couldn't identify it.

'Or someone very good at sneaking up on people. Someone renowned for stealth.'

'Like?'

'Like an Elf. God damn it! The Elves. It was them all along! No wonder they keep popping up all over the place! Hiring me to help them indeed! Princess, can I borrow your landus?'

She nods. We're at the Palace grounds and soldiers and guards rush up to surround the Princess. I take a swift leave, dragging on the reins and sending the horse racing back the way I came.

I had been meaning to call on Cicerius and pick up some payment, but it'll have to wait. Is it today or tomorrow I have to pay my debt to the Brotherhood? I can't remember. Too much excitement. Too much all-night rioting.

The Elves have gone from Truth is Beauty Lane. I run through the ornamental gardens and hammer on Lisutaris' door. When a servant answers I run right over him and find Lisutaris consoling herself with her water pipe. Fortunately she doesn't yet seem to be too stoned.

'Lisutaris, I need a favour, and quick.'

'Very well.'

'Can you tell me where a couple of Elves are now?'

I describe them to her. Lisutaris closes her eyes for a few minutes. An expression of tranquillity settles on her face. My nose wrinkles at the powerful smell of thazis in the room.

Her eyes open. 'They're at Twelve Seas docks. Boarding a ship.'

She's a powerful Sorcerer, Lisutaris, Mistress of the Sky. Pity she smokes so much. I impinge on her for another favour, which she again is willing to grant, aware that I saved them all in the riot. So minutes later I am thundering through Turai on a fine horse from her stables, on my way to intercept two treacherous Elves.

The streets are chaotic. Rubble lies everywhere. Municipal horse carts are starting to collect the bodies but there are still plenty left to choose from. The streets to the south are flooded from a burst aqueduct. Steam rises in the burning sun. It takes me a long time to get down to Twelve Seas and I'm sweating and cursing by the time I'm in sight of the docks.

A giant figure strides in front of me, grabbing the reins and bringing me to a shuddering halt. It's Karlox, of all people.

'So you survived the riot,' he growls. 'Good. You got another three hours to pay up.'

'Karlox. You are dumb as an Orc and you have no idea how much you annoy me.'

I swing a hefty boot and catch him full in the face and he goes down in a heap. I spur my horse on, struggling through the hopeless crowds of Twelve Seas, many of whom have been burned out of their pitiful dwellings. There are huge gaps in the skyline where the six-storey slums have collapsed into smouldering rubble on to which municipal firemen are still pouring water. My horse is starting to protest. In the heat it finds carrying my bulk quite a difficult task. We struggle on.

'Thraxas!'

It's Makri, sword in one hand and a bag of manuscripts in the other. She's on her way to her mathematics class.

'Makri, you are a madwoman. There won't be any classes today. The Guild College is still on fire and the Professors are probably all hiding in their cellars, unless they're dead . . .'

She looks disappointed.

'Are you sure?'

'Of course I'm sure. Now, if you want to be in on the end of the case, get up on the horse.'

She leaps aboard. The horse protests some more. No doubt Lisutaris will be able to nurse it back to health.

'Where are we going?

'The docks. I'm chasing the Elves. They've got the Cloth. Probably the dwa as well.'

Makri finds it hard to believe that the Elves are criminals. 'Callis is a healer.'

'He'll need healing when I get through with him. Can you think of anyone better qualified to sneak up unnoticed behind Hanama and Sarin? And don't forget the way the Elves mysteriously appeared when Sarin had us cold outside the city. They'd been following us. They've used me all along, Makri. Representatives of an Elf Lord indeed. They're after the Cloth for themselves.'

'Crooked Elves?'

'That's right. I was a fool to take them on face value.'

Makri asks me why I didn't check their credentials in

the first place. 'Because they handed over a load of money of course. Now, stop asking stupid questions.'

We're next to the harbour. Just as well as the horse absolutely refuses to take another step. We dismount and look around. Several ships have been sunk in the harbour and a few more are smouldering at their berths. Only one vessel seems to be in good shape and the captain is obviously keen to get out of the city fast because he's preparing to weigh anchor as we approach.

He looks at us curiously: a large fat man, ragged and filthy, dripping with sweat, and an exotic young woman with a chainmail bikini and a sword sticking out from under her cloak.

'Travelling far?' he says.

'Not travelling at all,' I reply. 'Just looking. For Elves. Any aboard this ship?'

He stares at me blankly, the universal sign in Turai that a bribe is called for. I pass him a guran.

'Just got on,' he says. 'Cabin at the front. We're sailing in three minutes, with you on board if you're still here.'

Makri and I rush along the deck past various surprised-looking sailors who are making ready to cast off. Most of them are bruised from the riot but work away busily. You have to be tough to sail these seas.

There's only one cabin door at the end of the ship – most passengers on a trader like this would simply bunk down wherever they found an empty piece of deck – and we kick it open and stride right in. I'm not prepared for what we find and am rendered temporarily speechless.

I unsheathe my sword almost involuntarily, although there is obviously no one here to fight with. No one here at all except two dead Elves, each with a knife deep in his heart. They've both been stabbed in the chest, I mean; I'm not absolutely certain if Elves' hearts are in the same place as ours. They're dead anyway.

I catch a momentary flicker of sadness passing over Makri's face at the sight of the young healer dead on the floor, but she's too hardened to death to show much emotion. Myself, I'm not sad at all, but I'm sure as hell puzzled. From the lack of outcry outside I presume that no one on the ship knows what's happened, but it can't be an easy thing to kill two Elves without making the slightest sound. I study the weapons. Small throwing knives, unleashed with murderous accuracy before the victims knew what was happening.

'Looks like they met their match in sneaking,' I grunt, and start searching the cabin.

They've stashed the dwa under their bunks. There's no sign of the Cloth. A call comes from the ship's mate that they're about to sail. I'd like to take the dwa but it's not strictly necessary and I don't want to draw attention to myself by struggling off heavily laden. I notice the healer's pouch lying spilled open on the floor. There's a few lesada leaves among a bunch of other herbs. I pick them up and stuff them into my own pouch.

'Shame to waste them,' I tell Makri. 'Very good for hangovers.'

'You don't have to explain, Thraxas. I never expected you to have any qualms about robbing the dead.'

We leave the cabin and stroll off the ship as though nothing has happened.

'Shouldn't we inform the Captain his passengers are dead?'

'What for? Just make trouble all round. For two dead

Elves the authorities will be crawling all over the ship. It'll be weeks before he can sail. And we'll be answering questions from the Guard for a month. This way he gets to dump the bodies out at sea as soon as they're discovered. I expect they already paid for their passage. And he's got six bags of dwa to make up for his trouble. Much easier all round.'

I'm more tired than a man should be. I have difficulty walking home.

Large parts of Quintessence Street are unrecognisable, mere burned-out shells. The municipal carts haven't got round to collecting the bodies from Twelve Seas yet, so the place is quite a mess. The Avenging Axe is badly damaged but at least it survived. When Gurd went mad and started swinging his axe around not many of the locals fancied talking him on.

I walk in, climb upstairs and fall asleep on the remains of my couch.

Karlox has a nasty cut on his face where I kicked him. I know, because he's standing over me with a sword in his hand.

'You ever consider knocking?' I growl.

'Door wasn't locked,' says Karlox.

I'm still lying on the couch. The point of Karlox's sword is making it awkward for me to rise. He's got five men with him. They're looking for the money I owe. I don't have it.

'The Orc bitch went out,' grunts Karlox, reading my mind. I was hoping she'd burst in and rescue me. 'Got the money?'

'On its way. I'm just waiting for payment to arrive.'

Which is true. Cicerius owes me plenty for clearing his son, and clearing the Princess. I can't really explain this to Karlox however, and I doubt it would make any difference if I could. For Karlox it's more fun if I don't have the money.

'Got a spell ready?' he asks, knowing full well that I haven't.

'No? Not much of a Sorcerer, are you? Not much of anything really. Apart from a gambler. A bad gambler. Very unlucky. And this is the most unlucky day you're ever going to have, fat man.'

One of his thugs laughs. They advance and stand round me, swords drawn.

'What is going on here?' demands a now familiar voice. It's Cicerius. I never thought I'd be so pleased to see him. He strides into my shattered room, a grim frown on his narrow face.

'Well?' he says, going right up to Karlox and looking him squarely in the face. This is a little awkward for Karlox. Not only is Cicerius much too important for him to push around, but the Traditionals use the Brotherhood as muscle during the elections.

'Some private business, Praetor,' says Karlox, uncomfortably.

'The gambling debt, no doubt,' says Cicerius.

Of course. I forgot everyone in the city knew about it.

Cicerius motions to his attendant. The attendant draws out a purse, counts out some coins, and hands them over to the Brotherhood enforcer.

'Depart,' orders the Praetor.

Poor Karlox. He's sadder than a Niojan whore at this turn of events. He was looking forward to doing a little enforcing on me. He departs, followed by his men.

I rise, grateful at this turn of events, and thank Cicerius. He looks at me with disapproval and gives me a brief lecture on the stupidity of gambling, particularly if I'm not good enough to win.

'The money will be deducted from your fee.'

Praetor Cicerius, looking more incongruous than ever in his crisp white toga in my shattered room, informs me that the Princess has been cleared.

'The Consul has been reliably informed that the dragon was in fact killed by Orcs from their Embassy. An

internal Orcish power struggle, apparently. The Civil
Guardsmen picked up their bodies here in Twelve Seas.'
None of this is true, of course. It's just the story
circulated by Bishop Gzekius to clear the Princess's
name, as promised. 'The Orcish Ambassadors are not
happy, but as several of their Orcs were found in a place
they were forbidden to enter, a church, they cannot
protest too much. The King is relieved to learn that his
daughter has not been indulging in illegal activities. It's
a satisfactory outcome I don't suppose it's true?'

I tell him no, it isn't and fill him in on most of the
details, including everything I know about the Bishop's
misdemeanours. The Praetor is shocked to learn the
extent of the Bishop's machinations. I imagine Gzekius
will find his influence at court waning from now on. Of
course Bishop Gzekius will now have it in for me in no
uncertain fashion so it won't hurt to have Cicerius
ranged against him. Despite being troubled by what I tell
him the Praetor has to admit that I've done what I was
hired to do. The Princess is in the clear. Soon everyone in
Turai will hear rumours that the whole trouble was the
fault of the Orcs trying to steal the Cloth. There's some
truth in that, I suppose. They did start it when they hired
Glixius to get it for them, although events quickly
spiralled out of his control.

The Praetor informs me that he has already let it be
known to the Niojan Ambassador that his attaché
Attilan was killed by the rogue Orcs after he stumbled
on their criminal activities. Clever of the Praetor. Gets
Turai a bit of breathing space. Nioj will still destroy us
one day.

Whether it was the Pontifex I saw at Attilan's house or

the Elves that killed the attaché, I don't know. The Elves, I think. Now that the Orcs have been blamed, it doesn't seem to matter much.

'Of course our Elvish allies who sent us the Cloth are not fully satisfied. We may have shifted the blame for the theft on to the Orcs but there is still no sign of the Cloth. Do you know where it is?'

I shake my head. I've been expecting Cicerius to give me a hard time about this – I haven't forgotten Consul Kalius accusing me of lying – but he seems quite prepared to believe me.

'Well, I cannot expect you to do everything. I am already grateful to you for keeping my son out of court and preserving his reputation. And that of the Prince. However undeserved that may be.'

He makes to leave, but halts at the door. 'Princess Du-Akai wishes me to pass on her sincere gratitude,' he says, and departs abruptly. As he opens the door the smell of smoke drifts in from the smouldering buildings in the street outside.

I muse on the Praetor's words. Not bad. The Princess likes me. Maybe I can do a little social climbing on the back of that. Anything to get out of Twelve Seas. Makri appears the moment he departs. Having returned half-way through his visit she has, of course, been listening at the door.

'Looks like your luck's changing, Thraxas. Everyone's pleased with you. The city officials, the Royal Family – even the Brotherhood is off your back.'

I nod. It's true. Things do look better than a few days ago. My enemies are either pacified or departed. Apart from Glixius Dragon Killer – with my luck he will have survived the riot – and the Society of Friends, who will no doubt be mad as hell at me for messing things up for them. I can live with that.

I stub my toe on something on the floor. It's a bottle of beer. Must've been hidden under the sofa. I open it and take a long swig, then stare out the window at the wreckage outside.

'Somehow you don't seem too pleased,' says Makri.

I turn to face her. 'I'm pleased enough, I guess.'

'Well you're looking as miserable as a Niojan whore.'

I take another drink. 'I don't like being given the run-around, Makri. Not by anyone, but particularly not by you.'

Makri raises her eyebrows. I tell her to stop acting innocent.

'The Association of Gentlewomen stole that Cloth, didn't they? Don't bother looking shocked and perplexed, you haven't been in civilisation long enough to fool an experienced liar like me.'

Makri continues to look shocked and perplexed. She denies any knowledge of what I'm on about.

'Oh yes? I've wondered all along what Hanama's involvement in all this was. The Assassins don't hunt for stolen goods, they assassinate people. It seemed just possible that they would've wanted the Elvish Cloth for their guild, to make their own magic-proof room perhaps, but in that case why was it always Hanama who kept appearing everywhere? Why not some other Assassin? There are plenty of them. Way too many in fact. But it was always her. And she's a difficult woman to shake off, as the Elves found out last night.'

Makri continues to be silent. I continue to talk.

'I knew immediately I saw the Elves that Hanama had killed them. A knife throw to their hearts before they could even move. Very efficient. Difficult to carry out, of course, given that Elves are practically impossible to take by surprise, and they move pretty damned quick when they're in danger. But not beyond the powers of Hanama. They only outsmarted her before because she was half drowned in the flood. I wondered at first how she could possibly have known it was the Elves – after all, I'd only just worked it out and I swear no one did before me – then I realised. I mentioned it to the Princess just before I went after them myself. And to Lisutaris. One of them got a message to Hanama, and fast. Quite a group, this Association of Gentlewomen, Makri. Princesses, Assassins, Sorcerers. And barmaids.'

I fix her with a stare.

'Are you suggesting I've been passing on information?' says Makri, not sounding too pleased about it.

'Well have you?'

'No, I have not. And if the Association of Gentlewomen has been pursuing the Elvish Cloth it's news to me. Why would they want it anyway?'

'Same reason everybody else in this city wants things. For money. You told me you needed fifty thousand to buy a Charter. Taking a collection box round Twelve Seas isn't going to get you far. But a nice fat thirty thousand for the Cloth will.'

Makri absolutely denies it. 'I don't even believe that Hanama is in the Association of Gentlewomen. She's an Assassin.'

'So? Maybe she feels she's not making out as well as she should. Held back from promotion by the men in the

Assassins Guild. And, now I think about it, when she came round on the beach she called you Makri. Struck me as pretty friendly at the time, for someone you'd only ever seen once before during a fight. And the Princess passes on her best regards as well . . .'

We stare at each other across the room. Makri strides over to me and sticks her nose right in my face.

'Thraxas,' she says, her voice clipped and hostile. 'You might be right about the Association. Maybe Hanama was getting the Cloth for them. I hope she was. We need the money. But I wasn't in on it. I wouldn't pass any information about your business behind your back, because you're the only friend I have in this stinking city.'

She glares at me angrily. I glare back at her. Seconds pass in hostile silence. It strikes me that I don't have too many friends in this stinking city either.

'You've been working too hard, Makri. Let's go downstairs. I'll buy you a drink.'

THIRTY-ONE

In the aftermath of the Eight-Mile Terror the violence that was gripping Turai fades into the background. The elections are still going ahead, and the Brotherhood and the Society of Friends are still struggling to control the dwa market, but in the face of the recent calamity most of the outright hostility is either toned down or suspended altogether. Everyone is too busy rebuilding the city, and rebuilding their lives.

Cerius is not brought to court, due to the evidence I present to the Consul. Prince Frisen-Akan's attempt to import narcotics on a large scale doesn't reach the ears of the public. Cicerius is pleased on both counts. Thanks to me he keeps his reputation. What's more, any sort of civic disaster usually unites the population behind the Royal Family, which will quite probably hand the elections to the Traditionals. Too good a politician to miss an opportunity, he makes a fine series of speeches in the Senate, urging everyone in Turai to pull together to rebuild the city. It does his election chances no harm at all.

The Renowned and Truthful Chronicle of All the World's Events notes that one of the sad losses to the city in the recent riot was one of its most powerful Sorcerers, Tas of the Eastern Lightning, found dead in an alley with a crossbow bolt in his back. The paper laments the fact that a mad rioter could have acquired such a weapon. It didn't take Sarin the Merciless long to get rid of him.

'I guess if you've extorted ten thousand gurans, it's better not to have to share it,' said Makri when she hears the news. 'Are you still keen to meet her again?'

'Absolutely. The sooner Sarin comes back to Turai the better. I could do with some reward money. I'll soon show her who's number one chariot around here.'

The Avenging Axe is being knocked back into shape. Here, as in the rest of Twelve Seas, architects and builders are engaged round the clock to put things right. Workmen are busy everywhere, sweating in the heat. Flocks of stals, displaced by fire from their old perches, fight for nesting space on the roofs of the new buildings. The King opens the royal vaults to pay for much of the work, which is very generous of him, although cynics might say he was merely buying his supporters' victory in the elections.

Personally, I'm in good shape. A fat payment from Cicerius and an extra bonus from the Princess, not to mention the valuable double unicorn the Elves gave me as a retainer. Plus a solid reputation as a man who gets things done.

'So, are you moving back to Thamlin?' asks Makri, who is busier than ever, with thirsty bricklayers, roofers, glaziers and architects clamouring for drinks all day.

'Not yet, Makri. The Traditionals might think I'm a good Investigator but they don't want me as a next-door neighbour. It'll be a while yet before I'm invited back to the Palace.'

'Who's going to win the election?'

'Probably Cicerius. Which is good for me. Except Senator Lodius and the Populares now really dislike me.

Which is bad for me. I never have any problem making new enemies.'

In between shifts Makri has been studying hard and spends long hours in her room with her books and scrolls. Undeterred by her experience in the Fairy Glade, she's had her nose pierced again by Kaby. It keeps her happy.

I take out two necklaces, and hand one to her. She stares at it suspiciously.

'It's the Red Elvish Cloth we wrapped round our necks on the night of the Eight-Mile Terror. It worked pretty well then, so I asked Astrath Triple Moon to treat it with a spell which means we now have strong protection against sorcerous attacks. It's illegal to keep it, but now it's woven into these necklaces no one's going to know.

Makri puts it on. 'Not that I need it,' she says. 'I'll trust my swords against magic any day. But you could do with it. Try not to pawn it this time.'

'I'll do my best.'

Kaby and Palax wander in looking tired. They're busking on the streets again. I don't envy them. It's too hot to work. Fortunately, I don't have to. Not for a while anyway.

'Another "Happy Guildsman", if you please, Gurd.'

He passes over a tankard but I notice he's looking glum. 'Tanrose is annoyed with me,' he complains. 'She says I never pay her any attention. What can I do?'

'For God's sake, Gurd, don't you even know the basics? Take her some flowers.'

The ageing Barbarian looks puzzled.

'Flowers? Will that help?'

'Of course it will,' I state with confidence.

And it does.